ONCE UPON A DREAM

After her mother's death, New Zealander Delphine Rowe decided to go to London and stay with her cousin, Waldo, whom she had never met. When she arrived at Waldo's flat, there was a glamorous party in progress and Delphine felt out-of-place. When she finally found her cousin, he took her under his wing — much to the annoyance of his girlfriend, Charlotte. The next morning, Waldo introduced Delphine to his friend, Trevor, who eagerly made plans to entertain her. But, gradually, Delphine found herself falling in love with Waldo . . .

Books by Paula Lindsay
in the Linford Romance Library:

COUNTRY DOCTOR
AWAKE, MY HEART
MAGIC IN THE RAIN
DREAM OF DESTINY
SUDDENLY A STRANGER
THE GOLDEN GIRL

PAULA LINDSAY

ONCE UPON A DREAM

Complete and Unabridged

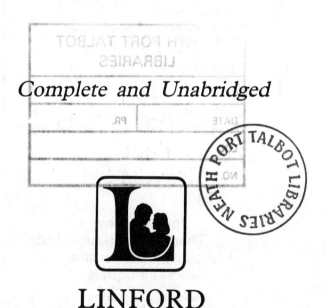

LINFORD
Leicester

First published in Great Britain

First Linford Edition
published 1997

British Library CIP Data

Lindsay, Paula, *1933*–
Once upon a dream.—Large print ed.—
Linford romance library
1. Love stories
2. Large type books
I. Title
823.9'14 [F]

ISBN 0-7089-5083-3

Published by
F. A. Thorpe (Publishing) Ltd.
Anstey, Leicestershire

Set by Words & Graphics Ltd.
Anstey, Leicestershire
Printed and bound in Great Britain by
T. J. Press (Padstow) Ltd., Padstow, Cornwall

This book is printed on acid-free paper

1

THE taxi turned into a small, cobbled street and drew to a halt. Delphine peered through the windows into the wet, dark night in mingled surprise and dismay, for this was not at all what she had expected to find at the end of her long journey.

"Are you sure this is the place?" she asked doubtfully, turning to the cabby.

"It was your bit of paper, not mine, miss," he returned indifferently. "Cranmer Court, South-West One you wanted, and this is it. I can't do better than that."

"No, of course not. Thank you." With a sinking heart, she opened the door and stepped down to the cobbles, hunting for her purse in the bag that was slung over her shoulder. "How much do I owe you?"

He named a sum that staggered Delphine. But she had no knowledge of prices in England and she was much too tired and unsure of herself to dispute the amount. She found a note and some silver, paid the cab-driver and stood watching as he executed a skilful turn in the narrow court and sped his taxi away and out of sight around the corner.

Delphine looked about her. It was no longer raining and a crescent moon was struggling through a thick bank of dark cloud. The small court was quiet in contrast to the bustling, brightly-lit streets that had seemed to throb with traffic and people. She was still not convinced that this was her proper destination. For this was not at all the kind of background that she had visualized for her cousin Waldo.

Cranmer Court had conjured up a vision of a beautiful old house set in its own grounds. Her imagination had quite run riot and she was finding it almost impossible to reconcile the dream with the reality. Having been born and reared on the other side of the world and possessing only vague ideas of her mother's country, it had not seemed incongruous to suppose that a stately home might exist in the heart of its capital city.

Apart from a few parked cars, the little court was deserted, but the sound of music stole across the night and there was a sudden burst of laughter from a brightly-lit upper window a few houses from where she stood. They were not exactly houses, she realized; more like garages with rooms above.

She checked the slip of paper which bore her cousin's address and made her way to the nearest doorway. There was an illuminated bell-push with a name-slip beneath but it was not Waldo's name. She moved on, checking each door until she finally found what she sought — the name of W. S. Guthrie, R.A.

With a racing heart, she rang the bell and then stepped back to look up at the lighted window as more laughter echoed on the night air. It seemed as though her cousin was giving a party. She was very thankful that he was not away from home, for then she would have been stranded with very little money and no friends in a strange country.

The door opened abruptly, startling her. A tall, blond young man grinned down at her engagingly. He was younger than she had expected and extremely good-looking. Suddenly consumed with shyness and a belated realization of the enormity of descending on an unknown cousin with very little warning, she stammered: "Mr. Guthrie — Waldo . . . ? I'm Delphine — "

"Come on in," he invited warmly, smiling down at her. He took her outstretched hand to draw her into the narrow hallway that only seemed to lead to a steep flight of stairs. "You're the girl I've been looking for all evening!"

She was puzzled, for she had not

4

told him exactly when she would be arriving and, as things had turned out, she had reached England much sooner than she had intended. She looked up at him hesitantly. "Is it a party?" she asked a little foolishly as the loud and heavy beat of music suddenly broke out above their heads.

"Of course — and the more the merrier," he said brightly, slipping an arm about her waist. "You don't know how glad I am to see you, darling . . . we're a little short on women and somehow I missed out on the deal."

Delphine did not want to offend him at the outset, but she did not care for his easy, confident familiarity and she was beginning to wonder if she had made a terrible mistake. She had been so determined to come to England, so sure that she would be welcomed with the kind of open-armed hospitality she had known all her life. Well, she was certainly being greeted with open arms but not quite in the way she had expected, she thought dryly. She extricated herself carefully from the encircling arm. Not at all offended, he beamed down at her happily and it occurred to her that he was slightly drunk.

"You do know who I am?" she asked impulsively, suddenly doubtful.

He nodded. "Sure I do — you're Delphine!" he said confidently. "Come on up and say hello to everyone!"

She still hesitated. "My case — ?"

He looked down at the heavy suitcase, noticing it for the first time. Surprise touched his eyes and then he chuckled. "You mean to make a night of it, obviously," he said lightly.

"Oh, if it isn't convenient for me to stay — " Delphine began swiftly, dismayed and yet relieved.

He brushed aside the words with an easy smile, a careless shrug, and dumped the suitcase in a corner. "Leave it here for now," he said. "We'll sort it all out later. Come and have a drink."

Reluctantly, Delphine followed him

up the narrow stairway, simply because she did not know what else to do for the moment. She did not like him and she was apt to rely a great deal on first impressions. It was obvious that the flat or whatever it was would be much too small to house both of them and that she could not stay . . . and it was entirely her own fault for impulsively taking the first cancellation on a flight to London instead of waiting for confirmation that she would be welcome and that it was convenient for her cousin to house her temporarily.

The stairs led directly into a large room which seemed to be some kind of studio, for canvases were stacked against a wall or stood on easels at one end of the L-shaped room and the moon was now clearly to be seen through the enormous window in the roof. Heavy velvet drapes completely covered one wall, which Delphine guessed to be entirely made of glass. The farther end of the room was apparently designed for comfort and leisure with its television set, hi-fi unit, leather seating around the walls and the bar that was at present doing brisk business.

It seemed to Delphine that a sea of hostile faces were turned in her direction — and then she realized that it was indifference rather than cold hostility. She was a stranger, a not very striking stranger, and of little interest to that insular, confident and very glamorous gathering. Almost immediately everyone turned back to their conversations, their flirtations, their enjoyment of another of Waldo Guthrie's parties.

There were not so many people present as Delphine at first supposed but it was very noisy and confusing. A sudden surge of music from the group with their vibes, drums and guitars completely drowned whatever it was that her companion said as she clutched instinctively at his arm. After all, he was her kin and she relied on him to look after her in this strange new world.

She looked up at him helplessly. "I'm so sorry . . . I didn't hear you."

He shrugged, detached himself and left her, thrusting his way through the press of people towards the bar. Delphine supposed that he had gone to get her a drink which she really did not want. She felt very awkward and self-conscious, standing alone in her travel-creased suit and low-heeled shoes among all the fashionable dresses and exquisite coiffures that adorned the other women in that room. She was most unsuitably dressed for a party but she had neither expected nor wanted a party to welcome her to London . . . and, of course, it was merely a coincidence that Waldo had chosen to entertain his friends on this particular evening.

She wanted to run but she was only too conscious that she had nowhere to go. She was not impressed by her first dealings with her famous cousin but at least he was a straw to cling to in the surging flood of uncertainty. But, looking anxiously for him, she saw that he had been claimed by a girl who slipped her hand into his arm and smiled at him with dark eyes. Delphine suspected that she was already forgotten by the man who was proving to be such a disappointment.

She could do nothing but wait until he remembered her existence, she thought wearily . . . and she turned away to stare blindly at a canvas that was propped against a chair. No one was taking the least notice of her and yet she could not help feeling that she was under attack by a battery of curious and amused eyes.

Tears welled to her eyes. She had travelled across the world to be met with such cavalier indifference by a man who was her only surviving kin, and she was abruptly convinced that she should never have left her native land and all the dear and familiar people and things which meant so much to her. She had no home, no money, no job and no friends in England, and she did not know where to turn now that Waldo was failing her.

Her tense figure attracted the notice of the man who was responsible for the canvas that she seemed to be studying so intently. He gazed at her, frowning, trying to place her but very sure that he did not know her and wondering who had brought her to the party. She seemed to be alone, oddly forlorn. After a moment or two he walked quietly across the room to her side.

She seemed to be wholly unaware of him or her surroundings, so preoccupied was she with her thoughts. Not very happy thoughts, he decided. He bent his head to look into her face and was taken aback to discover that her blue eyes were drowning in tears that threatened to overspill.

He did not wish to embarrass her. So he said wryly: "I'm sorry you feel like that about it." He had a deep and very attractive voice, warm and vibrant.

Delphine turned her head slowly. She looked at him, hearing the words without really registering them. Then she recognized compassion in his eyes, kindly warmth in his smile — and she was abruptly furious with her cousin for exposing her to the evident concern of this tall stranger. "I don't know what you mean," she said flatly.

"The painting . . . I'm afraid you don't care for it." He indicated the canvas.

"Oh!" She resented him for having dragged her thoughts unwillingly back to the reality of the present. "It's awful!" she announced and turned her back on the colourful, bizarre painting that she had not really seen for all her gazing.

"I thought it wasn't to your taste," he remarked, a little amused. "But that kind of thing is popular just now, you know. I don't think we've met before, have we?"

She looked up at him briefly. He

was very tall and his dark hair was crisp and curling to his collar. He had the rather romantic style of good looks that Delphine associated with portraits of the Victorian era and the formal elegance of his clothes seemed to emphasize the likeness. There were a few silver strands woven among the dark curls and there were little lines about his eyes, lines that her mother had always described as laughter-lines. He had a humerous mouth and eyes that seemed incredibly blue against the healthy tan of his skin. When he smiled he was strikingly, even dangerously, attractive and Delphine knew an odd little lift of her heart that alarmed her. She swiftly decided that he was the kind of man who expected every woman to be flattered by his interest and to fall promptly into his arms. Very sure that no man should be quite so handsome, she said brusquely: "I've only just arrived in this country, so we couldn't possibly have met before."

She looked for her cousin with a

hint of desperation in her eyes. It had been a long day and she ached with weariness. It scarcely seemed possible that anyone could be so thoughtless as to dump her among a crowd of strangers and promptly forget all about her when it must be obvious that she was nearly dropping with exhaustion.

"Isn't anyone looking after you?" he asked, undeterred by the tone of her reply. "You don't appear to have a drink . . ."

"Waldo went to get one, but obviously he's been side-tracked," she said impatiently. "You don't know where he is, I suppose? I can't see him anywhere."

There was a slight pause. Then he said slowly: "Do you mean Waldo Guthrie?"

"Yes, of course! This is his party, isn't it? You must know him," she returned edgily, too tired to care if she was being rude.

"Yes, I do know him rather well, as it happens," he said a little dryly. "I suspect that I know him much better than you do."

"Very likely!" Delphine retorted sharply. "We've just met for the first time and he isn't at all what I expected. But as I don't know anyone else in this country I mean to cling to him like a limpet until I find my feet. He's my cousin."

The faint frown that had lurked in his eyes was suddenly swept away. "I have the oddest conviction that you are Delphine Rowe," he said then.

She turned to him in swift relief. "Oh, then Waldo has told you about me! Do you know, I was beginning to believe that he didn't know me from Adam!"

"As far as I know, he hasn't talked about you at all," he returned lightly. "But that's probably because he thought you were settled in New Zealand and had no idea that you'd turn up out of the blue."

"But he was expecting me! I wrote to him," Delphine explained. "I sent him a photograph, too, so that he'd know what to expect!"

"Then your letter must have gone astray," he suggested. "It does happen."

"Oh, I can't believe that!" she protested immediately. "When I told him my name just now on the doorstep he didn't seem at all surprised. Ah, there he is now, talking to that dark-haired girl."

The man by her side followed the direction of her anxious glance and raised a quizzical eyebrow. "I doubt if your name meant anything at all to that young man," he said easily.

Delphine turned to look at him in dismay. "You can't mean that!"

"I'm afraid I do," he told her, smiling.

Her face clouded suddenly. "He did say something peculiar about my luggage," she said slowly. "I wondered if he was quite sober, actually. And it is odd that he simply walked off and left me with scarcely a word and hasn't bothered about me since. Do you think he really doesn't realize that I'm his cousin from New Zealand?"

"I imagine he would be astonished to hear that you are his cousin from New Zealand," he told her. "Although it's certainly possible that the Edmundsons have relatives in that part of the world, I think it would be stretching coincidence too much, don't you?" She raised a bewildered face and he smiled suddenly and held out his hand. "I should have introduced myself — and certainly I ought to have realized your likeness to your mother much sooner. I am your cousin Waldo."

Her eyes widened. "You!" she exclaimed.

"Am I such a disappointment?"

"Oh, no! You're a decided improvement on the man I mistook for you!" she returned bluntly and with feeling.

"I am compelled to agree with you," he said, eyes twinkling. "But tell me what you're doing in London, apparently on your own."

"Throwing myself on your generosity,"

she said frankly. "You are all the family I have left now and I thought we ought to know each other."

"Your mother . . . ?" he said quickly, concerned.

Her mouth quivered but she answered steadily: "She died two months ago."

"I'm sorry," he said gently. "Truly sorry. I wish I'd known, Delphine."

"It was all in my letter," she told him quietly.

"The one that went astray," he returned. "Most annoying . . . for one thing, this isn't at all the kind of welcome I would have wished for you."

"Am I welcome?" she asked.

"Of course you are!" He smiled down at her. "I shall be glad to have you cling to me like a limpet for as long as you wish."

Waldo Guthrie was decisive and quick-thinking, and he acted swiftly on his decisions. Delphine was surprised by his flair for organization, for she had grown up with the belief that the artistic temperament did not walk hand in hand with an ability to manage one's affairs very well. Her gifted father had proved that many times. Living in a world entirely his own, he had been the most impractical of men, content to leave everything to the capable care of the wife who loved and understood him and never allowed herself the luxury of criticizing his lack of interest in the world outside his book-lined study. Nicholas Rowe had been a brilliant man, sensitive and erudite, a historian who wrote about history as it should have been. But his books did not find a ready market and there was little enough money to keep them all. All his wife's efforts, all her economies throughout the years, had not provided more than a very small income for herself and her young daughter on his death. Delphine was sure that the strain and stress of eking out that income had led to her mother's lingering illness and premature death.

But Waldo was obviously a very

different man to her father for in an amazingly short time she found herself tucked up in bed, refreshed and renewed by a hot shower and thanking her cousin for the tray he had brought, complete with snowy napkin, shining cutlery and one perfect rose in a cut-glass vase.

She looked at him half-laughing, and asked: "Do you just wave a magic wand . . . or what?"

"I expect it's a gift," he said, the smile in his eyes robbing the words of all conceit.

"I hope it rubs off on me, then!" Delphine exclaimed. "I'm not very efficient, I'm afraid. It may be that I sent my letter to the wrong address, for example."

"It doesn't matter now that you're here, does it?" he said kindly. "Eat your supper and settle down to sleep and we'll talk in the morning."

She nodded. "I'm keeping you from your party," she said ruefully. "I won't be at all popular with your friends."

"I doubt if I've been missed," he told her. "I hope the noise won't keep you awake. These affairs tend to go on till the early hours."

"Nothing could keep me awake!"

He smiled, believing her, for she was obviously utterly weary. He paused by the door to look at her. She was slight and touchingly frail, he thought. She sat very upright in the narrow bed, carefully balancing the tray before her. Waldo had been very young when his cousin Alexandra left England to settle in New Zealand with her husband but her fragile loveliness had left an indelible impression. He wondered now if this girl's slenderness and vulnerable air had touched a chord in his subconscious, reminding him of the affection and admiration he had felt for her mother. For although he had absolutely no claim on his interest, he felt an oddly protective responsibility for the young woman whom he had never met until tonight.

"Are you sure that there's nothing

else you need?" he asked.

"Nothing at all! Now do go back to your friends," she urged. "I don't want to be a nuisance to you, you know."

He smiled and went away without further comment, and Delphine, spooning soup with appreciation, wondered if he already thought of her as a nuisance, an inconvenience in his obviously busy and well-organized life, and if he would have cabled to tell her to remain in New Zealand if her letter had reached him. He had assured her that she was welcome to stay until she chose to make other arrangements but Delphine could not free herself of the uncomfortable conviction that her unannounced arrival had left him without any alternative.

Suddenly dispirited, she recalled that he had whisked her very quickly from the presence of his friends once he knew her identity, as though he was embarrassed by her unexpected descent on a bachelor abode. She supposed it was unconventional for her to stay with him, however temporarily, but she had never imagined that he lived alone, looking after himself; she had been so sure that he must live in an enormous house with a host of servants.

He was, in fact, her mother's cousin, still a boy when her parents married. Perhaps it was too precarious, too remote a relationship on which to base even a small part of her new life. She wondered if she had taken too much for granted in supposing that Waldo Guthrie would gladly give her a home and take on a degree of responsibility for her simply because some of the same blood ran in their veins . . .

Waldo went back to the party which was running perfectly well without him. He went to the bar and poured a drink and stood looking down at the amber contents of his glass for a few moments, his thoughts still with the girl who occupied his guest-room.

He wondered if it had been practical or wise to make her so welcome, cousin or no cousin. His life was very full, both socially and work-wise. He had not the time nor truly the inclination to nursemaid a young girl who was very much a stranger in a strange country. He wondered why she had left New Zealand, which was her home and where she surely had friends. It could not simply be that sentiment had urged her to seek a long-lost relative, he thought cynically. She had admitted that she had very little money left after paying her air fare . . . and hastened to add that she meant to look for a job at the first opportunity and did not expect him to support her. Disarmed by her quiet frankness, Waldo wondered now if he had been deceived by a wistful air of innocence.

Of course, she might not be particularly interested in him or his wealth, he conceded. It could simply be that he was able to pave the way for her, introduce her into the right circles and provide her with the opportunities to secure the kind of future she wanted for herself. Yes, perhaps he had been a little too swift to assume the mantle of virtual guardianship of an unknown cousin.

Charlotte Rivers detached herself from the group of people who were earnestly discussing the psychic versus science controversy that was currently in the news. She made her way across the room to join Waldo.

They were more than friends and not quite lovers, the gifted and very handsome artist and the beautiful, coolly confident journalist. They had met when Charlotte kept an appointment to interview him for her newspaper, some months before. Waldo had turned the tables and interviewed her, with the result that they had become close friends who were often to be found in each other's company and yet laughingly dismissed any suggestion that they meant to marry.

Waldo was a light-hearted lover who had no desire to become seriously involved, no interest in a permanent relationship with any woman . . . and he made it clear at the outset to any woman who responded to his overtures. He liked the company and appreciated the charms of a beautiful woman but he liked his freedom very much more — and could always plead that a dedicated artist such as himself did not expect any woman to be content with second place in his life.

Charlotte, like many another woman before her, believed that in time he would reconsider his verdict and sensibly settled to play the game his way for the time being. She was as light-hearted as he could wish, made few demands on him and never made the mistake of showing possessiveness or jealousy if he smiled on another woman. Their relationship had lasted for several months and Charlotte sometimes allowed herself to hope that he might marry her eventually. She was not deeply in love with him but she did want to marry him, if only to prove to the world that she had the power to make

Waldo Guthrie change his mind about marriage.

She smiled at him now. "A charming little waif," she said lightly. "Who is she, Waldo?" She was much too shrewd to pretend indifference when the whole room had buzzed with speculation about the girl who had been whisked away so abruptly by Waldo.

"I'd have introduced you, but Delphine is very tired," he returned smoothly, knowing very well that Charlotte was eager to know all there was to know about his unexpected guest. "She's only just arrived from New Zealand," he went on. "She's my cousin — come to stay with me for a few weeks. I've been expecting her for some time. Didn't I mention it?"

"She's staying with you?" Charlotte echoed with the faintest lift of her eyebrows.

He met her eyes levelly. "Certainly."

"Won't that make life a little difficult for you, Waldo?" she said with a wry smile.

"Oh, she won't intrude on my private life," he replied confidently.

"Well, I think you'll find that she cramps your style a little, darling," Charlotte warned lightly.

"You're afraid that she might cramp your own style, my dear Charlotte." His blue eyes regarded her with amusement.

"Nonsense!" she declared. "I don't allow anyone to get in the way of what I want, Waldo."

"And you want me?" he suggested, slipping an arm about her waist.

"For the moment," she agreed blithely. "I shall tire of you eventually, of course — but just now you amuse me."

His arm tightened about her abruptly. Careless of their surroundings, careless of watching eyes, he bent his head and kissed her. He acknowledged that he wanted her and that until passion died, as it inevitably would, he would continue to want her. Charlotte was very beautiful. She was also sensitive and intelligent. He was not possessive or demanding and he did not feel that she belonged to him in any way. He merely asked that they respected each other's privacy and independence. So far she had never questioned how he spent his leisure hours when they were not together. He admired her and liked her and they shared an understanding that he valued. If he had been a marrying man he might have thought very seriously of asking Charlotte to be his wife.

It was late when the party finally came to an end and the quietness of Cranmer Court was shattered by the echoes of good nights and laughter and the revving of car engines.

Delphine was abruptly woken out of a deep sleep and she was momentarily confused, staring into the greyness of the unfamiliar room in the early dawn. She lay very still, foolishly alarmed, and then, when her heart had quietened, she threw back the covers and padded on bare feet to the window.

Her cousin's home was more extensive

than she had realized and the small but comfortably furnished room allotted to her had once been some kind of an attic, she surmised. The dormer window overlooked damp roofs and a huddle of chimney-pots and in the distance was a tall, easily-identifiable tower . . . Big Ben, proving that she really was in London, England. The other side of the world to Wellington.

She shivered slightly, wondering if such an enormous step had been wise and asking herself what she really knew of her famous cousin. He was a very successful artist, of course. He was a very wealthy man for he had inherited family wealth from his mother and a title from his father that he apparently did not use. He appeared to be kind, courteous, charming. He was undeniably handsome and undoubtedly popular. He was also incurious for he had asked almost nothing about her and had apparently taken her completely on trust when she might be an impostor, for all he knew. But then, if he was taking her on trust, certainly she was also taking him very much by the same token. Alone in a strange house with a strange man in a strange city, she suddenly felt very young and vulnerable. She told herself firmly that she was being silly, that she surely had nothing to fear from a man whose eyes smiled so readily, that she was quite capable of taking care of herself in any eventuality.

Much too wide-awake now to go tamely back to bed, Delphine pulled on a towelling robe and knotted it about her waist. She would go down and make herself some tea. Waldo had shown her where the kitchen was and had also assured her that she must make herself thoroughly at home.

She closed the door of her room quietly and went downstairs. The house was very quiet and she supposed that Waldo had gone to bed. Not knowing what had woken her, she imagined that the party had ended some time before and his friends gone away although the house was still ablaze with light. She had been carefully schooled in economy and it went against the grain to ignore the light switches as she passed them. But she told herself firmly that it was not her house and perhaps her cousin liked to leave the lights burning.

She went into the kitchen, filled the electric kettle and switched it on to boil. Dirty glasses and plates were piled in the sink, food littered the table and overflowing ash-trays had been dumped haphazardly. She looked about her, wondering if she ought to clear away the debris of the party or if Waldo would dislike it. He had told her that he employed a daily woman to cook and clean and no doubt things had been left for her to deal with when she arrived.

The state of the kitchen caused her to wonder what the studio looked like and she crossed the hall to investigate . . .

Waldo ran his long fingers through his dark hair and smiled at Charlotte.

She had kicked off her shoes to curl up on a sofa, her full skirts billowing about her. She smiled back with lazy, provocative eyes.

"They're a good crowd, but it's been a long evening," Waldo said ruefully. He set down his glass and walked over to where Charlotte sat. "Perhaps I've been too impatient to have you to myself," he said quietly. He stooped to kiss her.

Charlotte's arms went up and about his neck. Murmuring his name, she drew him down and he caught her in a close embrace . . .

Delphine, walking in so innocently, checked on the threshold with an involuntary exclamation. Embarrassed and dismayed, she turned swiftly to leave — and collided with a low table so forcibly that the glasses standing on it were sent flying.

2

DELPHINE did not pause to explain or to apologize. She fled to her room and hurtled into bed and drew the covers about her and closed her eyes tightly to erase an image which seemed indelibly engraved on her mind.

She was not shocked, of course. He was a man of the world, an attractive man, a man who would obviously have women friends. Even so, Delphine could not go back to sleep. She lay taut and tense, half-expecting Waldo to come to her room to explain that it was not convenient for him to house her, after all. She was almost tempted to pack her things and steal out of the house before he could ask her to leave and she wondered if he would care, if he would be sorry, if he would feel any concern for her — a stranger in a city that was cold and unfriendly, without money, without a roof over her head, without friends.

She had just managed to drag herself out of the deep trough of self-pity when a light tap at the door set her heart hammering with trepidation. But it was not Waldo. A plump woman with a crown of thick auburn plaits and a cheerful face came into the room with a tray of tea. She introduced herself as Mrs. Grundy, told Delphine that breakfast would be ready in half an hour and announced that it was a beautiful day, the first day of spring . . .

The sun was shining but Delphine had not even noticed. The sky was blue and quite cloudless and London from her window did not seem so grey and dull and disappointing as it had on the previous evening. Her spirits were lifted as she looked out over the rooftops. It was all so very different — but exciting.

She bathed and dressed and brushed her hair. She studied herself in the mirror, debating whether or not she needed make-up to face the new day — and finally admitted to herself that she was a terrible coward, merely postponing the awkward moment when she must meet her cousin once more.

Waldo glanced up briefly as she entered the room, wished her a courteous good morning and went back to reading his newspaper. Delphine slipped into a chair opposite him, poured herself a cup of coffee and reached for a slice of toast that she did not want. She stole a glance at him and decided that a certain grimness in his expression did not encourage conversation. She did not know what to talk about, anyway. What did one say to strangers at breakfast?

She toyed with the toast, lacking appetite. For Waldo was silent, intent on his newspaper, virtually ignoring her. She fancied that he was wishing her back on the other side of the world.

Waldo, in fact, was merely interested

in the article he was reading — a clever piece of cynical journalism put together by Charlotte and he did not feel that he needed to stand on ceremony with his unexpected guest. He attributed Delphine's silence to shyness and a courteous reluctance to interrupt his reading and he would have been dismayed to learn that she was fretting over her intrusion of the night before.

He had been furious at the time, but only briefly, for he had instantly acquitted her of wilful intent, and very soon he had discovered an element of humour in the incident. The poor girl — blundering her way about a strange house in the middle of the night. No doubt she had been extremely embarrassed.

Charlotte had laughed with him and helped him to brush up the broken glass and told him not to embarrass his guest with any mention of the matter . . . and within minutes he had escorted her down to her car and kissed her a warm good night which thanked her for her tolerance and understanding.

He put aside the newspaper now and poured fresh coffee for himself. "What do you mean to do with yourself today?" he asked lightly, wondering if he could really neglect the canvas of the moment to look after her. He ought to work and he wanted to work, but it seemed a little unkind to ignore her obvious claims on his time and attention.

"I think I should look for somewhere to live, don't you?" she returned quietly.

He raised an eyebrow. "You have somewhere to live. Here. For as long as you wish."

"You can't want me to stay — !" she began impulsively and then colour swept into her face as she saw amusement flicker in his eyes. "I'm so sorry about last night," she blurted, conscious of her flaming cheeks. "I mean, I had no idea — "

"How could you? But if you are to stay, Delphine, then I think I ought to acquaint you with some of the basic facts of a bachelor's life," he said, teasing her gently, his eyes twinkling.

"Please, you don't have to spell it out," she said abruptly, embarrassed. "Obviously, you have friends and you've always been free to entertain them how and when you like." He laughed aloud at her choice of words and she stared and then a reluctant smile tugged at her own lips. "I mean — oh, you know what I mean!" she declared swiftly, rebukingly, half-laughing. And they were no longer strangers.

He put his hand over the small, clenched fist as it lay on the table. "Forgive me. I ought not to tease you," he said, smiling. "But last night's little incident does have its funny side, you know, in retrospect."

"Not for me!"

"Oh, surely . . . !" he protested swiftly. "No sense of humour? I don't believe it, Delphine!" He put his strong fingers beneath her chin and tilted her face. "That mouth betrays you, my dear."

The touch of his hand and the smiling warmth of his blue eyes did the strangest things to Delphine . . . an odd little sensation trickled up and down her spine and her head swam slightly and there was a sudden tingling in her veins. She thought he was going to kiss her — and she panicked, jerking her chin from his firm fingers. She saw surprise leap to his eyes and she forced herself to smile . . . a shaky little thing but a smile that obviously reassured him.

Waldo was unused to having women jerk from the touch of his hand and he was slightly disconcerted. But she was obviously unsure of herself and still very shy; cousins they might be but they had yet to become friends, he reminded himself.

"Oh, what a beautiful morning!" The resonant tones of a trained baritone preceded the entry of one of his oldest friends. "Oh, what a beautiful day,"

Trevor sang cheerfully as he walked into the room and pulled out a chair from the table. "Just in time for breakfast, am I? Good morning — and it really is a good morning at last, isn't it?"

Mrs. Grundy followed him into the room with fresh coffee and a clean cup and saucer, used to his ways. Waldo nodded to his friend. "And why did you fail me last night?" he demanded.

Trevor laid one long finger against the side of his nose in a sly little gesture . . . and winked. "A prior engagement," he said lightly, grinning. "Prior to coming along to the party — but somehow things didn't work out according to plan."

Waldo eyed him thoughtfully. "You mean that things did work out according to plan," he said dryly as Trevor sugared his coffee, reached for the toast rack and then butter and marmalade. He turned to his cousin. "Delphine, I am forced to introduce Trevor McLean, but please don't notice him too much.

Pretty girls go to his head like wine!"

Trevor laughed. "Very true," he agreed, and smiled at Delphine. "And you are a very pretty girl," he said warmly. "Where have you been hiding all my life? Delphine, eh? French?"

His eyes, warm and friendly, smiled into hers and she smiled back. It was impossible not to like someone so likeable, not to be attracted to someone so attractive, not to respond to someone so responsive to oneself. "I'm a New Zealander," she said easily. "I think it is a French name . . . my mother liked it."

"So do I," he said promptly.

"Delphine is my cousin," Waldo enlightened his friend, dispelling any false illusions about her presence at his breakfast table. "She only arrived in England last night and I'm giving myself the pleasure of entertaining her for a while."

Delphine's mouth suddenly quivered and swift, betraying laughter flickered in her eyes, for his choice of words, following on that earlier conversation, could have been happier. Their eyes met and held briefly and she saw that he shared her amusement. He smiled — and she felt that they were friends, after all.

"Cousins! That's a relief," Trevor said gaily. "So I won't be poaching on your preserves if I offer to show Delphine the sights?"

"Not at all," Waldo assured him carelessly.

Trevor turned to Delphine. "Is this your first visit to England?"

"Yes, it is . . . and there's so much that I want to see," she said impulsively.

"Rely on me," he said promptly. "Waldo is much too busy to be courier, you know. Whereas I am a gentleman of leisure and entirely at your service."

She hesitated briefly, glanced instinctively towards Waldo who sent her a little nod of reassurance, and then said warmly: "You're very kind, Mr. McLean. Thank you!"

"Trevor," he corrected firmly.

She smiled. "Trevor," she agreed obediently.

Waldo pushed back his chair and rose to his feet. "I'll leave you to work out an itinerary," he suggested lightly. "I shall be in the studio if you care to wave on your way out."

Before he closed the door, they were eagerly making plans for the day. Waldo was pleased that Delphine showed no signs of shyness where his friend was concerned. It would be difficult for anyone to be shy with Trevor, of course. He had a happy gift for putting people immediately at ease. He was good-natured and easy-going and extremely kind and Waldo knew that he would take a genuine delight in looking after Delphine and showing her the sights of the city. Thus he was released from some of his responsibility for her and could turn to his half-finished canvas with a clear conscience.

Delphine liked Trevor McLean. He promised to be good company and he had all the energy and enthusiasm and cheerful disposition of youth combined with an attractive degree of maturity which assured her that he would take good care of her. She had found a friend, she thought happily.

And indeed, like old and dear friends, they strolled hand in hand along Whitehall and paused to admire the Horse Guards before walking on to feed the pigeons in Trafalgar Square. Delphine trailed her fingers in the blue waters of the fountains and craned her neck to stare at Nelson on his column. They wandered through St. James's Park and watched the ducks on the lake. They saw guardsmen parading in the forecourt of Buckingham Palace and Trevor pointed out the Royal Standard fluttering in the breeze. They lunched in a little Greek restaurant that Trevor knew near Victoria and did full justice to the excellent cuisine. They made their way back along the Embankment, passing the Abbey and the Palace of Westminster, which Trevor promised they would explore another day, and finally stood on Westminster Bridge in the shadow of Big Ben to admire the sweep of the river on its way through the city and the beautiful dome of St. Paul's Cathedral in the distance.

Trevor put an arm about her shoulders and smiled at her. She was very sweet; almost child-like in her delight at everything they had seen and done. He had lived in London all his life and yet he had seen it through new eyes that day.

"Nice, eh?" he said softly.

"Oh, it's so beautiful!" she exclaimed, a little emotionally. It was strange that a country she had never known could suddenly seem like home. Even more strange that a city which had seemed so cold and unwelcoming one day could be so warm and friendly and delightful only the next. But she knew that she had Trevor to thank for the change.

She had really enjoyed the day. They had talked incessantly, laughed with each other, enjoyed each other and their surroundings . . . and she felt there could never have been a time when she did not know him. Now, standing on the famous bridge with the slate-hued water flowing beneath them on its way to the sea, his arm about her, she felt that they were very close and her heart warmed to him. Impulsively, she kissed his cheek as he stood beside her, his head on a level with her own. "I don't know how to thank you," she said impetuously. "It's been such a wonderful day!"

He touched his fingers to the cheek that she had kissed and there was an odd sensation in the region of his heart that was vaguely disturbing. "You've just thanked me," he said slowly, meaning it. She looked up at him with a swift, sweet smile.

He took her home in time for afternoon tea — and Waldo threw down his palette and brushes, ran a hand across his eyes and returned to their world to lend an indulgent ear to the eager account of their day.

Even while she vied with Trevor in the telling of it all, Delphine dealt deftly with the tea things. She handled the heavy pot and delicate china with care and Waldo noticed with the eye of an artist that she had beautiful hands. He leaned back in his chair and studied her, intrigued by the dancing excitement in her eyes and voice, the laughing affinity that she had so rapidly reached with Trevor. He suddenly felt very much an outsider — and ridiculously old.

Delphine broke off abruptly in the middle of a sentence, suddenly realizing that he was not listening. "I expect we're boring you," she exclaimed lightly. "The unforgivable sin!"

It was very foolish but all her pleasure in the day suddenly evaporated as she met his enigmatic blue eyes and immediately realized his indifference to their activities. He could not really be interested in what she did or how she spent her days as long as she did not interfere with his life, his work, his pleasures — and she told herself firmly that it was a perfectly reasonable attitude.

She must not expect his interest and attention as well as the kindness of his hospitality. They were virtual strangers and she must seem very young and dull and insignificant to such a man. And, of course, he had all the demands of his work to consider. She recalled that her father had always retreated to his study and his own world and taken little or no interest in how she and her mother spent their time. Waldo was an artist . . . and it was an insular, isolated way of life. Yet it hurt just a little that he had so promptly handed her over to someone else's care, obviously thankful to be relieved temporarily of his responsibility for her.

"Not at all," Waldo returned courteously, wondering what she had seen in his eyes to make her shrink into her shell so abruptly. He felt an odd little spurt of resentment that she should be on the defensive with him and yet so swiftly at her ease with

Trevor — and hastily dismissed the foolish pang of something that was almost jealousy.

As Delphine went out with the tea-tray, Trevor quietly closed the door behind her and then strolled the length of the room to study the almost-finished canvas on the easel. "I like it," he said at last, having given it a close if not very critical scrutiny.

Walso glanced up from the careful cleansing of his brushes, a faint smile in his eyes. "I'm glad," he said, a little dryly. "I shall finish it with a tranquil mind now that it has the seal of your approval."

Trevor grinned, undismayed by the sarcasm. "Do you mean to paint Delphine?" he asked curiously, turning to look at his friend.

"I might. Why do you ask?" Waldo returned carelessly.

"The way you looked at her. I've seen that look before," Trevor said lightly. "You were mentally transferring her to canvas."

Waldo nodded agreement. "She has good bones," he mused with the artist's detachment. "Lovely lights in her hair. There's a certain quality that might be quite a challenge, though . . . yes, I think I should like to paint her, Trevor. But she might not wish to sit for me, you know."

Trevor looked sceptical. He had yet to meet a woman who was not flattered by the suggestion that a famous artist should paint her portrait and he did not think that Delphine would be any exception to the rule. "It must have been quite a surprise — a long-lost cousin turning up on your doorstep," he said slowly.

"She has told you?" Waldo laughed softly. "A very pleasant surprise, though. She's a nice girl, Trevor. Very much like her mother, too. I've been sorting through some old canvases today and came across one or two that might interest you." He indicated a pile of paintings that were stacked in a corner. "Have a look," he suggested.

Trevor turned them over. They were early products of Waldo's talent and he caught his breath in surprise as he realized that each painting, all of a woman in varying mood and pose, held some quality that reminded him instantly of Delphine's fragile prettiness.

"They weren't painted from life, of course," Waldo commented. "Alexandra left for New Zealand when I was only fourteen. But she obviously played a greater part in forming my artistic style than I knew at the time."

Trevor studied each canvas carefully. "I guess you were a little in love with your cousin Alexandra," he said shrewdly.

Waldo smiled. "Perhaps. Calf love can leave a lasting impression," he agreed. "I admired her very much and she was always very kind to me."

"I expect you feel that you've known Delphine all her life," Trevor commented, restoring the canvases to their former place against the wall.

Waldo hesitated. A little hint of wrynes touched his eyes. He supposed he ought to feel that Delphine was utterly and dearly familiar and perhaps he might if she did not seem determined to remind him that they were strangers, for all the fact of their kinship.

He evaded a direct reply. "She needs someone like you to keep an eye on her, Trevor . . . and I shall be happy to know that she's in good hands."

"Oh, I shall keep both eyes on her," he returned promptly. "Let her loose in London and there'll be a queue at the door. It's my good fortune that I happen to be first in line for once and I don't mean to give up my place to anyone!"

Waldo looked at him, half-smiling. "Take care!" he warned. "You'll be in love again before you know it."

"It's too late for warnings," Trevor said wryly. "I'm head over heels already. Waldo, I mean to marry your enchanting little cousin!"

Trevor had been in and out of love

a dozen times and his friends had learned to take little note of such declarations. But Waldo was struck by a new sincerity and determination behind the words and it occurred to him that Trevor might be in earnest this time. Strangely, he did not feel surprise. Seeing them together, he thought it inevitable that Trevor had fallen for the pretty and very appealing girl who had entered his orbit so unexpectedly. It was perhaps equally inevitable that Delphine should respond to the warm charm and attractiveness of his friend's personality . . . and she was not sophisticated enough to conceal that response.

"It had to happen," he said lightly. "You were bound to get your come-uppance one day. Well, I hope you get what you want — but isn't it a little soon to be talking of marriage? You only met this morning!"

Trevor smiled. "Oh, I won't rush her into anything," he promised. "I can rely on you not to repeat my impulsive words, old man? I hope I can also rely on you to describe me in glowing terms at every opportunity and thus further my cause," he added lightly.

"I shall certainly warn her that you're the worst rake in town," Waldo assured him, his eyes twinkling.

Trevor laughed. "Excellent! Most women find that a very attractive recommendation. Doesn't that explain your own popularity? But you're something of a reformed rake these days, aren't you?" he added, a little curiously.

Waldo smiled. "Old age," he said carelessly.

"Charlotte Rivers," Trevor amended shrewdly. "A beautiful woman . . . clever, too. A little too clever for me but exactly your style. Settling down, Waldo?"

"I very much doubt it," he returned easily.

"You wouldn't tell me if it was on the cards," Trevor observed. "You always did play a very close game."

"If and when I announce my intention to marry I shall be generally believed, don't you think?" Waldo replied.

"Touché!" Trevor conceded, laughing. "People are apt to fall about laughing whenever I talk about taking a wife, I admit. Still, I shall surprise them all this time."

"You're very confident," Waldo remarked.

Trevor nodded. "Love is very often a one-sided affair," he said thoughtfully. "Baffling, usually. The man cares and the woman doesn't — or she's crazy about him and he hasn't a single serious thought in his head about her. When it's mutual one has a certain feeling . . . a kind of amazement at such fantastic luck! Yes, I am confident, Waldo. But, as I said, I don't mean to rush Delphine into anything. I want her to be really sure — just as sure as I am!"

As the door opened, he turned swiftly and eagerly, and Waldo thought wryly that no woman, however inexperienced, could be blind to such betrayal of interest. Delphine's smile was swift and warm for his friend; strangely, Waldo's heart contracted a little, for that smiling warmth did not seem to extend to him. Thinking ruefully that for the moment he had ceased to exist for either of them, he covered the canvas and put away his paints and brushes with methodical neatness — and he was wholly unaware that Delphine was disconcerted by a seeming indifference in his manner.

He was so aloof, so detached, so cold in comparison with Trevor's easy, light-hearted warmth. Very much a stranger, whereas Trevor had become instantly her friend. She wished she could feel so much at ease with the man who was temporarily her host. She must soon look for a job and somewhere else to live, she told herself firmly. Waldo could not really want her to stay indefinitely.

It was very likely that only innate courtesy concealed his actual irritation at her invasion of his comfortable way of life. He obviously was only used to considering himself at all times. At the moment he was intent upon finishing a canvas and must feel little inclination to neglect his work for her sake.

It was foolish to be so sensitive to the hint of bored indifference in his attitude, she chided herself. Of course he was more or less indifferent to someone he scarcely knew and naturally he was bored by the eager enthusiasms of a first-time visitor to England, cousin or no . . .

Talking to Trevor, she was relaxed and confident. Waldo was in and out of the room, only casually joining in the conversation in passing. But when Trevor finally left after arranging to meet them for dinner at a well-known restaurant that evening, all Delphine's shyness suddenly flooded back.

She reached for a magazine and flipped idly through the pages, very conscious of the man who sat in a chair opposite, studying her with a faint smile. She opened the box on the low table at her side and took a cigarette she did not want and smiled rather abstractedly as Waldo instantly leaned forward to pick up the table lighter and snap it to flame.

"So you really enjoyed your day?" he asked, very sure that her thoughts were still with the man she had left with such obvious reluctance.

"Very much. Trevor is such good company, isn't he?" she said, more warmly than she intended.

"He's a great person," Waldo agreed. "You've made a conquest there, you know," he added teasingly.

"Oh, I don't think so," she demurred.

"He's just being kind, do you think?" His tone held irony. "To himself, certainly!"

Delphine smiled. "Perhaps he is a little interested," she conceded. "It's convenient for you — and very nice for me!"

Waldo frowned suddenly, laughter abruptly chased from his eyes. "Convenient for me?" he echoed slowly.

"What on earth does that mean?"

"I mean that I won't be a nuisance to you," she said frankly. "Trevor is very willing to take me out and about and he has promised to help me to find a flat — and a job, too. He knows so many people."

The careless words stung him suddenly and quite unreasonably to anger. "You are not a nuisance," he said brusquely. "Nor are you likely to be. I shall be happy to take you wherever you wish if you should care for my escort. There is no urgency for you to look for a flat — and if you are serious about taking a job then I have friends who can help in that direction. Enjoy Trevor's company and attentions by all means, but please don't imagine that you need to rely on him for anything. I am both able and willing to look after my own cousin, you know!"

She was taken aback, wondering what he had found in her innocent words to stir him to such annoyance.

"I didn't mean to offend you," she

said hastily. "You've been very kind, but you must have so many demands on your time, and I really am the uninvited guest, aren't I? You didn't bargain for someone like me arriving unannounced on your doorstep. And if I'd given myself time for second thoughts I don't think I should have thrust myself on you."

"I'm very glad that you did," he said firmly. "You seem to have fallen in love with London, but it is no place for a girl on her own unless she is very well suited to looking after herself. And I don't think that you are."

He turned away scarcely knowing why he had rebuked her so harshly. He had very little right to dictate to her so forcibly. Perhaps it had something to do with the odd feeling of responsibility that she had evoked from the very first moment of meeting. In all his life, he had never had to be responsible for anyone but himself and he had always preferred it that way. Yet something about Delphine stirred him to protectiveness and a most unaccountable tenderness.

He recalled that Charlotte had described her as a waif — and there was certainly an engaging air of wistful helplessness about her, a seeming need for the strong and reliable protection of a man like himself. A little alarmed by the avenue that his thoughts were unexpectedly turning into, he told himself sharply that Delphine was very probably a capable and competent young woman who knew exactly what she wanted from life and just how to go about getting it.

Delphine did not argue with him although she instinctively resented that ready assumption that she could not look after herself if necessary. Even as a hasty retort rose to her lips she realized the truth of his words. London was a big and bewildering city to a stranger.

She went to him and touched him on the arm. "I'm sorry if I seemed to be ungrateful," she said quietly. "I only wished to spare you any trouble, Waldo."

He looked at her, unsmiling. "I'm sorry to have given you the impression that it would be trouble."

Delphine gave a rueful laugh. "Oh, dear! I'm getting in deeper and deeper!" she exclaimed. "Do help me out!"

The merriment in her eyes was quite irresistible and her smile abruptly dispelled his irritation at her readiness to depend on Trevor. It was scarcely surprising, Waldo reflected, that Trevor was talking so soberly of marriage within a few hours of meeting her.

With a little shock, he suddenly realized that it would be easy to want her for himself. But he dismissed the foolish thought. She was much too young, too unsophisticated; not at all to his taste.

The smile in his eyes betrayed none of his thoughts as he looked at her. But there was a warmth in his gaze that impressed Delphine with sudden awareness of him. Her heart gave a foolish flutter and she turned thankfully as the door opened to admit Mrs. Grundy who had finished her day's work and was about to go home.

Waldo had some instructions for her and so Delphine took the opportunity to slip away. She went to her room to decide on a dress to wear that evening — and to wonder about that sudden anger in Waldo's eyes.

She had expected him to be thankful that she wanted a job and a flat of her own. Surely he ought to appreciate her reluctance to be a bother to him? Instead, he had taken swift exception to her words. Delphine could not help wondering if he felt some kind of responsibility for her because of their kinship, his boyhood affection for her mother and because she was alone in a strange country.

The thought that he might care enough to feel even a little responsible for her brought an odd glow of warmth to her heart. Holding one of her few long dresses against herself to view the effect in the long mirror, Delphine stared at herself with sober eyes. Waldo Guthrie was a dangerously attractive man, she realized. A girl like herself would be very foolish to ache for the excitement that she might find in his embrace. For she was not at all the type of woman that he admired.

3

DELPHINE decided on a simply-cut gown with a high neck and long sleeves, made of a dull gold silky fabric that flattered her slim figure. She piled her dark hair into a knot of curls on top of her head and threaded them with a silk ribbon to match her dress. She applied her make-up with particular care and then stepped back to survey herself in the mirror.

She would have had to be extremely naive not to know that she was looking her best, and her heart lifted unexpectedly at the thought that Waldo might think her pretty. She turned away from the mirror, took a deep breath and went down to join him.

As she entered, he looked up from a television programme on current affairs . . . and knew again that odd little shock as her youthful loveliness caught at his heart. Delphine would have been satisfied to know that indeed he did think her pretty. In fact, he knew a swift, compelling urge to kiss her . . . and rose from his chair.

He switched off the television set and turned to the bar. "What will you drink?" he asked casually.

"Just a small sherry, I think."

He looked at her, raising an amused eyebrow. "You've been warned about my cocktails?"

Delphine laughed. "All right, I'll have a cocktail," she agreed.

"Good. It's all ready for you."

She smiled but there was a faint disappointment that he had accepted her appearance so indifferently, for all her pains. For a brief instant she had fancied that she saw approval in his eyes, but the foolishness had been immediately crushed by the carelessness in his manner.

She sipped her cocktail and made an effort to talk to him lightly but she felt suddenly shy of the tall, very attractive man in the midnight-blue dinner jacket and frilled dress shirt of pale blue. He was really much too handsome, she thought wryly, wishing her stupid heart would behave instead of leaping about like a wild thing simply because he smiled at her.

"You look very nice," she said impulsively.

His smile deepened. "So do you," he said gravely. "I like that way you have of doing your hair. It suits you. Wear it like that when you sit for me."

Her eyes widened. "Sit for you? Do you mean that you want to paint my portrait?"

"Do you object?"

"Oh, no! How could I object? It's the nicest compliment you could pay me," she said hurriedly.

"Don't be too sure," he said lightly. "I haven't yet decided on the style. And you weren't too impressed with my moon goddess, remember." He strolled across the room to the canvas he mentioned, the brightly bizarre painting that she had stared at without seeing on the previous evening and castigated so rudely when it was brought to her notice. He glanced over his shoulder and caught the flicker of doubt in her expressive eyes. He laughed and said reassuringly: "Oh, I dare say your friends will recognize you! I want to make a start within a day or two and I shall want you to sit for me as and when the mood takes me, Delphine. I'll need you around for a few weeks at least, so don't find your flat too soon, will you?"

Delphine looked at him a little doubtfully. "Is that your usual method of working?"

"I have no usual method," he returned easily. "Each canvas dictates its own style, its own way of working. My portrait of you may be rather demanding. I shall need to study you thoroughly, know you inside and out. If you dislike the idea then you must say so, you know."

Delphine could not dismiss the feeling that he wished her to stay for reasons that were not wholly concerned with his surprising wish to paint a portrait of her. She felt a slight qualm and then, meeting the reasurrance in his eyes, she knew that she had no cause to distrust him and that he was motivated by a genuine concern. He was no doubt convinced that she would come to harm if he allowed her to leave his protection. So he had come up with this flattering but faintly ridiculous scheme and rather unconvincingly declared that he could not paint her portrait unless she was around to be studied whenever the fancy took him. She was much inclined to suspect that he had no real desire to paint her at all.

She believed that she was capable of taking care of herself but she did not deny that it brought a glow of pleasure to her heart to realize that he felt so much concern for her. Perhaps it was the forerunner of affection, she thought with an optimistic lift of that foolish heart — and hastily told herself not to be a silly, romantic idealist. He was a handsome, successful and sophisticated man of the world who could take his pick from a host of beautiful women. Was it likely that someone as insignificant as herself could ever steal into his heart?

She knew it was foolish and dangerous and promised to be a constant threat to her peace of mind but she heard herself warmly assuring Waldo that she would certainly stay until the portrait was finished. She sensed that he was pleased.

She was grateful for the degree of kinship which made it possible for her to stay beneath his roof without risking her reputation — and, conversely, equally grateful that their kinship was sufficiently remote for them to fall in love if they were destined to do so. At the same time, she was wryly convinced that even if she was destined to fall in love with her handsome, exciting cousin it was most unlikely that he would ever think of her in that way.

Her spirits lifted when Trevor hurried to greet them at the restaurant, admiration in his eyes as he turned to her and a faint implication of possessiveness as he took her hand and tucked it beneath his arm.

She was sure that she was completely cast into the shade when Charlotte Rivers arrived, strikingly beautiful in a starkly simple low-cut black gown. The gleaming auburn hair was coiled smoothly on her neck and there was supreme confidence in the glowing green eyes, in the bewitching smile that she bestowed on Waldo as he went to greet her, in the easy acceptance of his light, welcoming kiss. Delphine's heart sank quite foolishly and jealousy stabbed suddenly and painfully as she recognized the woman who had been in Waldo's arms just before the dawn . . .

Trevor gave a long, low whistle of apprecation and Delphine smiled, a little wryly. "She's very lovely," she said with a trace of envy.

"Very striking," he agreed. He smiled, reaching for her hand. "Not my style, though. I like a woman to smile at me just the way you do."

Her heart fluttered in sudden alarm. It was not so much his words but the way that he spoke them and the intensity in his gaze . . . she liked him far too much to want to cause him the slightest degree of heartache or disappointment. It would never do to encourage him to care for her when she was on the verge of loving another man. But she was not sure how one discouraged a man from loving when his liking and friendship already seemed much too valuable to give up.

"A slight change of plan," Waldo murmured as he escorted Charlotte through the tables to where Delphine and Trevor were seated. "We are not alone, after all. I asked Trevor and my cousin to join us. I knew you wouldn't mind, in the circumstances."

She did mind, for she particularly

enjoyed an evening with Waldo. He was the kind of man that any woman might delight to be with — handsome, attentive, excellent company and sufficiently well-known to ensure the right kind of deferential attention. She had hoped to lure him that evening into some kind of declaration, and she was not at all pleased to discover that she must share him. But she knew better than to betray her displeasure.

She glanced up at him, laughing. "Surely you haven't thrown that infant to one of the worst wolves in town!" she exclaimed. "What were you thinking of, Waldo?"

"My work," he said frankly. "I'm anxious to get a canvas finished in time for the new show. Trevor called this morning, met Delphine and promptly offered to look after her until she finds her feet. I was very grateful to him."

"I hope you'll continue to be grateful to him," she said dryly. "But I wouldn't trust Trevor McLean with such an innocent!"

"She's in safe hands," Waldo said confidently.

"I can't agree with you, but I suppose the girl isn't really your responsibility," she returned airily.

As they reached the table, Trevor rose swiftly to his feet, responding as almost every man did to Charlotte's glowing good looks and bewitching smile. Then, noting the flicker of satisfaction in her green eyes, he was annoyed that he had reacted so swiftly.

With faintly mocking gallantry, he caught her hand and carried it to his lips. "A superb entrance," he declared ironically.

Charlotte smiled but without warmth. "You always overdo it, Trevor," she retorted coolly. "And how are you these days?"

He was one of Waldo's closest friends and so they were frequently thrown together — and they successfully concealed the fact of a mutual dislike from everyone but each other. At first meeting, he had been antagonistic, and as he could have had no reason but an unaccountable dislike Charlotte had been baffled and annoyed and immediately determined to dislike him in return.

Waldo smiled at the light banter he took at its face value and then drew Charlotte's attention to the other member of the party. Delphine sat waiting to be noticed, feeling nervous. Waldo smiled reassuringly and put his hand lightly on her shoulder. "Charlotte, I know you've been looking forward to meeting my cousin . . . this is Delphine." Words and gesture covered Delphine with the warm mantle of his kindly protection and she glanced at him with swift gratitude in her eyes.

She was apprehensive because of the beauty and extreme elegance of the other woman. Her own gown suddenly seemed almost dowdy. She was nervous because Charlotte Rivers was a successful journalist who wrote a daily column in one of London's newspapers. She was sure that she could never hold her own in conversation with this clever and sophisticated woman. She was also embarrassed because the last time that she had seen Charlotte Rivers was during an incident that would stay in her memory for some time . . . and she was stupidly, foolishly and quite unreasonably envious of the woman's obvious place in Waldo's affections. But she was determined not to betray those innermost feelings, come what may.

Charlotte was immediately sensitive to the girl's discomfiture. She said lightly, kindly: "Oh, but we've already met — more or less! There's no need to be so formal, Waldo." Sitting down, she sent her glowing smile across the table to Delphine. "You were very elusive last night," she added. "You slipped away when I wanted so much to talk to you . . . "

She was referring only to Delphine's very brief and curiosity-stirring appearance at the party, being too good-natured to wish to embarrass her with any mention of that later and wholly accidental encounter. Too late, she realized that her words were misconstrued. Delphine blushed deeply and looked instinctively to Waldo . . . and there was swift, warm reassurance in his smile of response. Charlotte felt an odd little flicker of apprehension. She dismissed the fancy. Waldo was kind, warm-hearted, and he had always been a little sentimental about the girl's mother. It was probably very natural that he had assumed a degree of guardianship for the girl. Of course, Delphine Rowe was not such an inexperienced child as he seemed to suppose, Charlotte thought shrewdly — but she had no intention of setting him straight. For his cousin was a very pretty girl and there were obvious signs that Trevor had fallen a ready victim to her charm. Again, Charlotte felt a twinge of anxiety. It was true that Trevor had always been susceptible to a pretty face and an appealing air. But Waldo was a man like any other and it might damage their relationship if he began to regard his little cousin as an attractive young woman who merited more of his attention instead of an appealing child who only needed a little of his concern.

Delphine was encouraged by Waldo's smiling eyes to say lightly, dismissingly: "The circumstances didn't seem to lend themselves to conversation."

Charlotte admired the careless aplomb of the girl's reply but she wondered if it would have been so swift and so sure if she had not felt the moral support of Waldo at her elbow.

"Oh, I do agree," she returned easily. "Waldo's parties are always such noisy affairs that intelligent conversation is out of the question. He has some very old friends," she added, smiling at him quizzically. "But you'll find that out for yourself if you mean to stay with him very long."

Delphine wondered if she only imagined a slight note of disapproval in the last words. It could not conceivably be jealousy for Charlotte was obviously so secure in Waldo's affections that no other woman could even dare to dream of supplanting her.

She ought not to dislike the woman, she knew. Charlotte was friendly and very kind, very interested in hearing all about her life in New Zealand and the impulse that had brought her half-way across the world to England. The faint air of condescension might stiffen Delphine's spine but she reminded herself that the journalist was some years older and much more experienced and was probably only following Waldo's lead in treating her as little more than a child to be indulged.

It was irritating and she resented it but she tried to believe that it all stemmed from kindness. She ought to be grateful for the interest of a woman who might be useful to her in various ways in the future; and might also be Waldo's wife eventually, if she was reading the signs correctly, she thought bleakly. But she could not help feeling that Charlotte's friendliness sprang only from a desire to please Waldo and to impress him with her warmth of heart. It was not really natural for Charlotte to be so delighted that an unknown girl had turned up out of the blue to invade Waldo's privacy and encroach on the amount of time and attention he could spare from his work for his friends and his social life. Unless, of course, she was so sure of her hold on Waldo and the inevitability of their marriage that she was completely untroubled by Delphine's unexpected arrival.

Later, Delphine danced with Waldo, taking care not to betray her delight at moving in his arms to the slow, seductive music of the orchestra. The small floor was crowded and he held her close, so close that she was terribly afraid he must feel the rapid beating of her heart. He danced very well and their steps seemed to match perfectly and she was very tempted to give herself up entirely to the magic in his embrace.

She tried to tell herself that until the previous day they had been strangers for all that slight tie of blood. She had never seen him, known very little of him, thought of him with virtual indifference . . . and yet already he meant too much to her for peace of mind or heart. It was not only that he was very attractive and that her blood quickened at his slightest touch and that her heart contracted at his merest smile. There was a warmth and an integrity that endeared him to her so much. He was so very nice, she thought wistfully. It was very hard to accept that all the loving and wanting in the world must be in vain if a man had set his heart on someone else . . . and to the inexperienced Delphine his attentiveness to Charlotte and their obvious, warm intimacy seemed to be more than enough evidence that they were very much in love.

There might have been some small chance for her foolish hopes and dreams if they had met in different circumstances, she thought bleakly. As it was, he regarded her with the indulgent, vaguely affectionate tolerance that a man might feel for a younger sister.

"You're very quiet," he said when they had revolved about the dance floor for several minutes without exchanging a word.

She looked up, smiling. "I love to dance," she said. "We can talk at any time but I find it distracting when I'm dancing."

"Do you have to mind your steps so carefully?" he teased gently.

"Not with you — you're a marvellous partner," she returned promptly. "I should love to dance all night with you!"

He was amused by that disarming candour. It could be disconcerting but it was certainly attractive to a man who moved in circles where many dissembled with every other sentence and others seemed to think it foolish or unfashionable to voice genuine emotions and opinions. His young cousin was quite refreshing and really very sweet, he decided.

"I should be pleased to oblige you, but Trevor is sending me black looks already," he told her. "I think he and I would certainly quarrel if I sought to monopolize you."

"Charlotte would never allow it, anyway," she said bluntly.

He raised an amused eyebrow. "Charlotte is much too clever to protest if I danced with every woman in the place and ignored her for the rest of the evening," he said, his eyes twinkling.

"If you were mine I should protest!" she exclamed impulsively.

"That would be a mistake," he assured her.

"Perhaps. But I don't think I could help it. I wouldn't know how to be 'clever', as you call it," she said with rueful honesty. "I'm not very good at hiding my feelings, I'm afraid."

He looked down at her so thoughtfully

that she knew sudden panic. "I'm aware of that," he said quietly and her heart almost stopped at his words. Then he went on, smiling: "You've become very fond of Trevor in a remarkably short time, haven't you?"

Relief swept over her, for she was sure that she had nearly betrayed herself with those impulsive and very foolish remarks. It was dangerously easy to throw caution and discretion to the four winds when she was moving in his arms to slow and seductive music, naively supposing that the feeling within her must quicken some response in the man who held her so closely. But it was all very well to be near to loving when a man was free and far from indifferent, like Trevor. It was very foolish to cherish tender dreams of loving and being loved by a man like Waldo. Better that he should suppose her interested in his friend than suspect her growing feeling for him.

"You see, it shows!" she exclaimed, laughing. She did not need to lie. True, she had become very fond of Trevor in a very short time — and there was no need to explain that the affection she felt for one man bore not the slightest resemblance to the kind of emotion that another man had evoked without the least effort on his part. "I expect you think I'm much too impulsive," she went on easily. "After all, I only met him this morning. But I do like him, Waldo."

He nodded. It was not difficult to construe her use of the word 'like' as a shy reluctance to admit that she had fallen headlong in love. It did not surprise him. Trevor was a man of great charm and considerable attraction for women. Recalling his friend's reputation, he felt some concern — and then recalled that certain light in Trevor's eyes when he spoke of Delphine and how sure he had felt that this time Trevor was not just flirting. He told himself firmly that he need not fear for her peace of mind or happiness. Trevor would look after her perfectly well, and he would be released from all responsibility for his youthful cousin much sooner than he had anticipated. Considering how jealously he had always guarded his freedom and his privacy, it was a little strange that he was not better pleased by the prospect of regaining them.

"He likes you very much," he assured her levelly. "So it really doesn't matter if it shows how you feel about him, does it?"

The music stopped at that moment. Delphine walked with him back to their table, thankful that he was so unaware of the turmoil he caused in her heart with the supreme indifference of his words and manner.

Watching as he danced with Charlotte some time later, Delphine marvelled that she had dared to dream, even for a moment, that she might be a rival to that beautiful, self-assured woman in Waldo's arms. Deep in her being throbbed the growing conviction that she wanted him more than anything else in the world. And so, it seemed, did Charlotte.

"They make a handsome couple," she remarked "They are very close friends, aren't they?" The smile she sent to Trevor was just a little strained.

"They've been going around together for some months," he agreed. "It's lasted much longer than anyone expected, actually. Waldo usually extricates himself as soon as the gossips start speculating about his marriage plans."

Delphine felt a painful clutch of dismay touch her heart. "Does Waldo mean to marry her, to you think?"

Trevor shrugged. "I don't think any man ever means to get married," he returned. "But there comes a time when even the most determined bachelor finds himself thinking seriously about it." His eyes were suddenly intent on her face and his thoughts far from his friend's affairs.

It did not enter Delphine's head that he could be referring to himself.

Her heart sank abruptly at his words. He knew Waldo very well; they were obviously close friends; it was very likely that Waldo had confided his hopes and plans to him. She was suddenly convinced that Waldo did mean to marry Charlotte and that Trevor was well aware of the fact.

It was no more than she had expected, of course. But it was still a shattering blow to that fragile dream which persisted in haunting her stubborn heart. It was all so foolish. She scarcely knew Waldo . . . two days ago she had not even known what he looked like! She could not really be in love with him. No one fell so deeply in love so swiftly except within the pages of a romantic novel. No, she must not surrender to that fierce, compelling conviction that he was the only man in the world that she could ever love.

If she must fancy herself in love on the strength of a few hours' acquaintance, then it would be much more sensible to choose Trevor, who was just as attractive, just as charming, just as likeable and might be very willing to love her in return, she told herself firmly . . . and knew that loving had very little to do with common sense.

Seeing that she looked preoccupied, Trevor changed the subject. He was too skilful to press the point. He was very sure that the meaning in his words had not escaped her and he was content for the time being. But he did not mean to wait too long. For the first time in his life, he was determined to stay in love this time. He was sure that Delphine would marry him if he could sweep her into it before she had time to take stock of her emotions. He wanted her and he was grateful to the kindly fate that had brought her so unexpectedly into his life.

He suspected that she had led a sheltered life in New Zealand. He did not think there could have been any man of importance in her life. To his mind, she was ripe for falling in love with the first man who handled her gently and with expertise, and he did not mean to make any mistakes.

Nor did he make any in the following days. He was attentive and considerate, willing to spend as much time as possible in her company. It would have been impossible for anyone, however heavy of heart, to fail to appreciate him as a friend and companion or to fail to respond to the affection that he offered. Delphine grew more and more fond of him and foolishly supposed that his feeling for her stemmed from understanding and friendship.

Trevor did not attempt to make love to her, contenting himself with the occasional warm hug and the lightest of friendly kisses. He did not attempt to urge her into regarding him as a prospective husband. He simply set himself to win her lasting love and he was so confident of success that he was completely blind to the expression in her eyes whenever she looked at Waldo or spoke of Waldo. So he did not realize that she had been lost to him even before he knew that he wanted her.

Delphine was helplessly, hopelessly in love. It did not matter that Waldo was already in love with another woman, and therefore granting her very little of his time, attention or affections. She loved him. It was blind, compelling, irrevocable emotion that she neither questioned nor wholly understood.

She lived with the constant dread of betraying her feelings, yet could not bring herself to leave his house and his hospitality and remove herself from the close proximity that was torment. Her days revolved about Waldo. She rose in the morning, thankful for another day when she would see him, talk to him, have his company, however briefly. She went to bed at night with aching despair that another day had passed and brought her no nearer to the happiness that filled her dreams. She dared to dream because it was her only comfort and her happiness.

In her dreams, he loved her just as she loved him and only wanted that they should spend the rest of their lives together. In her dreams, loving him was wonderful, joyful. In reality, loving him was painful and difficult and foolish because he would never love or want her and the future was bleak and cold.

Waldo was aware of that inner turmoil and not in the least puzzled by it. She was young and in love for the first time and she was having some difficulty in handling newly-awakened and perhaps alarming emotions, he decided shrewdly. But Trevor was behaving very well. In fact, he was a little surprised by his friend's quiet and understanding selflessness. It was impossible to doubt that he was very much in love with Delphine. He did not attempt to hide his feelings or his desires. Indeed, he talked quite openly to Waldo, who was friend and confidant and could be relied upon to help in every possible way. Waldo was very willing to help but did not feel that it was necessary. It seemed to him that the relationship was progressing slowly but steadily towards an inevitable and satisfactory conclusion.

Delphine was still very shy and not wholly at her ease with him, Waldo realized. He understood that the gulf of age and background and temperament seemed too wide to be easily bridged but understanding did not entirely erase the vague hurt that she made so little effort to bridge it. He was not quite sure if she regarded him as a father figure or as a much older brother she had never really known and never really wanted to know, he thought wryly. He supposed he was a little stiff and impersonal at times, but she froze him with that continued shyness and that irritating reluctance to feel herself wholly welcome in his house and in his life. It seemed to him that she was determined to cling to the foolish fancy that he must regard her as a nuisance, and so he had given up trying to dissuade her of it.

At times, certainly, she was a nuisance, he told himself curtly as she invaded his thoughts once more when he was trying to concentrate on his work. He put down brush and palette and moved away from the easel, poured himself a drink and told himself that he must keep a much tighter rein on his own emotions if he did not want to discover that she was enchanting him also. It simply would not do, because she had set her heart on Trevor and it was not likely that he could ever capture it instead. It seemed almost an effort for Delphine to like him enough to be at ease with him, he thought wryly.

He was not to know that an entire day could be ruined for her because of a supposed lack of warmth in his smile, his voice, his manner. He was her weather-vane, swinging her from brief and ecstatic optimism to black despair and back again — and all without knowing or suspecting his power over her emotions.

★ ★ ★

Waldo threw down his pencils on a sudden surge of irritation. She was astonishingly and infuriatingly difficult to capture even in a preliminary sketch. A dozen different expressions, a dozen changes of mood in as many moments, were reflected in a face that betrayed almost her every thought to someone as perceptive as an artist needed to be.

Without analysing his reasons, he had postponed the portrait he had arranged to paint of her, merely explaining that he had too many other demands on his time to be able to give it the necessary attention. It was true that he had been busy with the exhibition of his work at a Bond Street art gallery and much involved with the subsequent publicity because of its success. But he had not been so busy that his fingers had not itched to pick up brushes and palette when a shaft of sunlight fell across her face or she turned her head so that light was reflected in her blue-black hair.

It was only when he finally admitted to himself that he was wary of the necessary involvement with his sitter which might sweep him into wanting her too much for peace of mind or body that he suddenly determined to get her on to canvas without further waste of time. If he was destined to love Delphine then all the procrastination in the world would not alter things. If he was merely consumed with physical and short-lived desire for her then he must clear it out of his mind and body with hard and dedicated work on her portrait.

She sat tense and still and anxious on the chair where he had placed her, obviously terrified of making the slightest movement, scarcely daring to breathe — and very likely wishing herself anywhere but the studio on this bright and sunny afternoon, he thought dryly. She was nervous and self-conscious but that was very natural and he had been prepared for it. She was also silent and he sensed a growing resentment; he supposed she would much rather be with Trevor instead of sitting for him. Perhaps she was regretting her impulsive agreement to their arrangement — a portrait in return for hospitality for an indefinite period. He was very near to regretting it himself, he thought impatiently.

Delphine started slightly as he moved away from the easel, throwing his pencils on to the low table with an impatient gesture. She was immediately wary, for there was a storminess in his eyes, a tautness about his mouth which she already recognized as danger signals.

She was very anxious to please him but she seemed to be failing miserably. He had made several attempts at the first sketches and each attempt had appeared to disappoint and infuriate him.

She did not know what he expected of her. He had simply sat her in a chair and arranged her in a variety of poses until he was satisfied and then surveyed her from a dozen different angles before picking up a pencil and beginning to work . . . and all with scarcely a word and nothing more than intent yet strangely impersonal concentration in his eyes.

She was stiff and cold despite the bright sunshine that streamed into the big room. Her neck ached because she had held the pose longer than was comfortable and he had not allowed her to rest. He did not seem to realize or to care that sitting so still for so long was an ordeal and she had been nursing a growing resentment at his lack of thought and consideration. She might love him very much but she did not mean to be blind to his faults, she told herself firmly.

"It's hopeless!" he snapped. "You seem to think I'm a camera! You may move, you know. I want you to move. Be natural. Be yourself. Talk, if you feel like it. But don't sit there like a blasted marble statue. I never paint still life!"

Colour rushed into her face. "I won't sit here at all!" she flared, leaping to her feet. "I've had enough!" She put both hands to her aching neck and rotated her head to ease the cramped muscles, wincing. "I didn't know it would be such a painful business or I wouldn't have agreed to sit for you at all!"

The outburst had relieved his tension and he was swiftly contrite. He went to her, belatedly realizing how long she had been still and how stiff she must be. "It wouldn't be painful if you'd relaxed and moved your head occasionally, you silly girl," he told her, half-impatiently, half-indulgently.

He pushed her back into the chair and put his hands on her neck, massaging away the tension and the pain.

"You didn't tell me I could move," Delphine said bitterly. "I thought I had to sit as still as possible . . . ouch, you're hurting!"

"Cruel to be kind," he said firmly.

"You'll be fine in a few moments. Just relax."

Delphine's heart was pounding and there was mounting excitement in her blood at his very touch, his very nearness. She was terrified that he would realize the effect he was having on her senses and she told herself for the umpteenth time that it was madness to stay beneath the same roof as this man. They lived in a close intimacy that made it impossible for her to crush the wanting of her heart and mind and body . . . and that same intimacy which somehow kept her firmly at a distance impressed on her continually that there was no future at all in wanting him, in loving him.

She was too incensed to relax, Waldo thought tolerantly. Caught up in his own thoughts and feelings, besieged by a desperate anxiety to get her on to canvas and out of his blood, he had swept on, making sketch after sketch and quite oblivious to her discomfort. He had been very much at fault. He should have made it clear what he wanted of her. In fact, it might have been better if he had not attempted formal sittings but simply sketched her at odd moments when they were together and relaxed in the easy, companionable intimacy of daily living.

It was not her fault that he was having so much trouble with her portrait, he thought wryly. It was not her fault that he was so emotionally involved that he could not bring clear, unbiased perspective to his work.

He smiled down at her. "I'm sorry, I didn't mean to be so hard on you," he said ruefully. "But you're extraordinarily elusive. I knew it would be hard to pin you down but I didn't expect it to be this difficult."

He stilled his hands, allowed them to rest lightly on her slender shoulders. Looking down at the small, flushed face and the soft, tremulous mouth, he knew the sudden impulse to kiss her. He firmly suppressed that impulse. It would be very foolish to cross the invisible line which made it possible for her to remain beneath his roof. One kiss, however innocent, might completely destroy the trust she obviously placed in him. It might pique him that she seemed to look upon him as a father figure while Trevor, much his own age, was regarded as a gay and youthful cavalier, but it was very much to his advantage.

For he had every opportunity to know her better, to study her thoroughly, to acquaint himself completely with her character. He might tell himself and others that he could not do justice to his artistic gift without an intimate knowledge of his subject, but in his heart he knew that he really needed time to decide how he felt about Delphine and what he must do about it.

For one incredible moment, Delphine had thought he meant to kiss her. Her heart lifted with indescribable hope and happiness. Then he straightened, removing his hands from her shoulders and turning back to the easel, and her heart began to beat hard and heavily, choked with disappointment.

His eyes had looked deep into her own for a long, tense moment. Eyes that were deeply, dangerously blue and so impossible to read. To him, she was merely a model for a portrait, she thought bleakly — a very irritating model who was hard to capture and who knew so little about sitting for an artist that she invited cramp and weariness and boredom with her ignorance.

He studied the last abortive sketch with thoughtful eyes, hands thrust deep into his trouser pockets. Delphine said quietly, impulsively: "It isn't going to be any good, Waldo. You don't really want to do my portrait at all. Your heart isn't in it and that's why you are finding it so difficult. You are painting me for all the wrong reasons."

He turned his head and raised a quizzical eyebrow. "And what are my reasons, do you suppose, Delphine?" he asked smoothly.

"To keep me here, of course."

He was surprised by the words. "That sounds as though you are here against your will."

She coloured, bit her underlip. "I don't mean that, Waldo. It's just . . . well, you don't really want me to leave here, do you? I've forced a certain responsibility on you and you're afraid I might come to grief out in the evil world on my own."

He looked at her steadily. "I thought you were content to stay here," he said, a little stiffly. "But if you prefer to be independent, then find your flat."

Delphine's cheeks flamed at the brusqueness of his tone. She realized that he was hurt and there was a heaviness about her heart. He was so good, so kind, so generous — and she had offended him with a seeming ingratitude. It must have seemed like a slap in the face. She cursed the impulsive tongue that had given Waldo the impression that she wanted to leave the warm and friendly hospitality of his home when in fact she wanted desperately to stay, close to him, despite the foolishness of a heart that loved him more with every passing day and only invited heartbreak because of it.

"I'm very happy here," she said carefully. "You have been very kind . . . "

"And it's stifled you?" he suggested swiftly, perceptively.

If only he knew, she thought wryly. But he was right to some degree. There was something stifling to a loving heart in a kindness that sprang from innate goodness rather than a deeper desire to cherish and protect. "I think I'm stifling you," she returned, taking refuge in turning the tables. "You like your privacy and your freedom. Having me around must be an awful nuisance."

"Have I encouraged you to think so?" he asked bluntly.

She shook her head. "Oh, no! Your manners are impeccable," she returned, thinking of the cool courtesy which kept her always at a distance when she ached for a warmer, deeper intimacy between them.

"Must you make it sound like a fault?" he said mockingly. "However, stay or go . . . I shall still want to paint you. I refuse to be defeated."

There was nothing in his tone to imply any real interest in her movements. Delphine hesitated briefly and then swallowed her pride. "I should like to stay," she said quietly.

Her reward was the swift smile that he sent her — the smile that had quickened many a woman's heart. "Good," he commented lightly, as though he had not been waiting on her decision with an anxious heart. "Now let's try once more — but promise me that you'll relax this time!"

He caught up his pencils, pinned a fresh sheet of paper to the easel and began to draw. This time there was no delay, no hesitation, scarcely any difficulty, but he was far from satisfied and had to content himself with the reminder that it was merely a preliminary sketch.

Within minutes, it was done — and he stood back to contemplate his work. He gave a little nod of partial satisfaction.

"May I see?" A little shyly, Dephine went to stand beside him. She stared at the swift, skilful sketch of herself with a feeling of surprise. "You make me too pretty!" she exclaimed impulsively.

"But you are pretty," Waldo said carelessly. "Doesn't your mirror tell you so?"

"Sometimes," she admitted.

"Only sometimes?" he teased. "You are too modest, Delphine. You should know that I only paint beautiful women." He smiled into her widened, startled eyes. "I've embarrassed you. But surely I'm not the first man to tell you that you're very lovely?"

He tilted her face with his fingers beneath her chin, for suddenly she was refusing to meet his eyes and he was

108

intrigued and faintly challenged. He was also irresistibly tempted despite all his firm resolution and he might have kissed her then if she had not abruptly pulled away with a rueful laugh.

"Oh, they queue at the door to tell me!" she declared, taking refuge in levity for she had been dangerously near to putting her arms about him and touching her lips to the warm, smiling mouth.

"They will when this portrait is shown," he assured her. "The whole world will want to know my lovely cousin."

Delphine wondered if he deliberately stressed the relationship. To her it seemed remote, but he often spoke as though the blood tie was greater than it really was. Perhaps he sensed the stirring of her emotions and wanted to discourage her, she thought bleakly. It did not occur to her that he sought to remind himself of the reason for her presence in his house at moments when he was most inclined to forget it.

4

CHARLOTTE could not understand why Waldo's young cousin was so popular with almost everyone who met her. For her part, she firmly believed that Delphine Rowe was an opportunist and far from being the innocent she seemed and she was amazed to discover that everyone else was apparently blind to the fact.

Waldo had been gulled into giving the girl a home for as long as she wished. Trevor had become hopelessly infatuated in no time at all, which implied that Delphine knew just how to get what she wanted, for all her youth and apparent naivety.

It did not matter to Charlotte, of course. But it was irritating to see grown men so taken in. Trevor's world seemed to revolve about the girl these days, and even Waldo, for all his knowledge of women, seemed to be ready to believe anything the girl told him about herself.

Delphine did not appear to need anyone to pave the way into society, Charlotte thought dryly, but Waldo wanted her to take the girl under her wing and so to please him she introduced Delphine to certain of her friends, took her along to her own hairdresser and the small, exclusive shops which she patronized, ushered her through certain doors that might otherwise have been closed to a newcomer and played the part of friend and adviser whenever necessary. She found that Delphine was very interested in journalism and was eager to hear all about Charlotte's own job and wondered a little wistfully if there might be some kind of opening for her in the same profession. Charlotte promised to look out for a likely job for the girl and privately thought that Delphine was not going to need to work to support herself. It was obvious that she would soon achieve the ambition that had brought her half-way across the world in the first place — the status and security of marriage with a wealthy man. It was scarcely surprising that Charlotte occasionally felt a spasm of acute dislike for the girl.

Charlotte had been seeing less of Waldo lately, and although it would not be fair to blame Delphine for his neglect when she knew perfectly well that he was extremely busy with the new exhibition of his work just now, she could not help a twinge of anxiety at times. After all, Delphine was living in his house and they saw a great deal of each other — and Waldo had never been immune to the attractions of other women. Delphine might easily be tempted to exchange the affections of one man for the other if the opportunity arose. Waldo was certainly a much more attractive prize than Trevor. Charlotte doubted if Delphine was really the type to make a lasting impact on Waldo, but one never knew.

She did not voice her disquiet and she had always been very careful to avoid even the slightest hint of possessiveness in her dealings with Waldo. So she befriended his cousin and pretended to like her and smiled on her friendship with Trevor and did what she could to encourage that relationship. Stifling her resentment of Waldo's lack of attention, she made a point of encouraging the interest of other men and accepting invitations that she had previously refused. There were many other men who found her attractive and sought her company. She was determined that the world would suppose it was her default rather than Waldo's if their relationship came to an end.

They still saw each other, of course . . . for a meal, at one party or another, at the homes of mutual friends. But the magic had fled from their affair — if there had ever been much magic in it, she thought wryly.

They were together one evening, dining at a favourite rendezvous after a film premiere, when Trevor and Delphine walked in, hand in hand, so absorbed in each other that they almost passed the table where Waldo and Charlotte sat without seeing them. Waldo rose, smiling and affable, and promptly invited them to join forces. Charlotte was annoyed but she did not show it. She offered a welcome with a warmth that matched Waldo's own and seconded the invitation.

Trevor looked to Delphine for guidance and saw the shining eagerness in her eyes . . . and accepted the invitation.

Charlotte realized instantly that he was very reluctant to join them. She did not blame him, for she had never counted Trevor McLean among her friends and she seldom bothered to conceal the dislike and antagonism which was returned in such good measure. There was really no reason for her to dislike the man and she had certainly never given him cause to dislike her, she reflected; but there was simply not an ounce of sympathy between them and neither was prepared to pretend.

She sent him a polite smile and received a curt little nod of greeting in return. Suddenly, unexpectedly, she was rather piqued, for she was used to swift admiration rather than indifference even from Trevor, who had never been able to conceal a grudging admission of her beauty. And she was looking her loveliest that evening, she knew. But Trevor had scarcely looked her way. He had eyes only for Delphine, in the new dress that Charlotte had helped her to choose only the day before. Charlotte acknowledged the girl's prettiness and she had been quite unable to suppress a natural desire to help her make the most of her looks and figure, but suddenly she was furious with herself for having advised Delphine to take a dress that bestowed a new and striking sophistication upon her. For not only Trevor but Waldo, too, was gazing at her with admiring eyes . . . and the girl was basking in their admiration. Men were such fools!

She was silent while the others exchanged light, empty, non-sensical banter, struggling with her annoyance and very tempted to get up and walk out on Waldo, who seemed to have forgotten her existence. She knew it was a ridiculous jealousy with very little foundation but she could not thrust it out of her mind.

Waldo sensed her withdrawal and was briefly puzzled. It was not like Charlotte to be silent and unsmiling on such occasions and he wondered if she felt tired or unwell. She had already told him of her hectic day and last-minute rush to keep their appointment. She had enjoyed the film and seemed her usual vivacious self when they mingled with friends in the cinema foyer before and after the performance, and when they eventually arrived at the restaurant she had appeared to be completely relaxed and happy.

He did not think she resented the arrival of the others. She seemed to have become quite fond of Delphine and they were friends. As for Trevor, Waldo privately thought that their supposed dislike of each other was a little game that amused them both. He was very sure that Trevor liked and admired Charlotte much more than he was ever prepared to admit . . . and he did not believe that there was anyone in the world that Charlotte could dislike. She was much too warm-hearted and extremely tolerant of faults and failings in everyone.

He rather thought he understood the reason for the shadow that touched her eyes. She was wryly aware of the delight that Trevor and Delphine found in each other, the obvious happiness and confidence in the future. Perhaps Charlotte was ultra-sensitive to their mood this evening. He knew that she had been expecting him to suggest marriage for some time and he had certainly been guilty of allowing her to suppose that it was in his mind. He realized that she did not love him and did not really want him to love her. But that might not prevent her from envying Trevor and Delphine. Even a man like himself, who had never wanted to commit himself so completely, so irrevocably, to that kind of loving could feel an odd tug at the heart, a strange, nostalgic yearning for something that he had never known.

Feeling a sudden sympathy for Charlotte, he reached out and clasped her hand and smiled into the green eyes that turned so swiftly to his face . . . and was rewarded with a very sweet, slightly rueful smile and a responsive pressure of her slender hand.

Delphine saw that brief exchange and her heart contracted. She might be very well aware of the love that they shared and its inevitable outcome but it could still jolt her heart every time that she received a painful reminder.

She could not compete with Charlotte; she had known that immediately. She was all that Delphine had always wanted to be. But she could still know a wistful envy deep down for the easy confidence, cool elegance and perfect loveliness that epitomized Charlotte and made her the obvious choice of love for a man like Waldo.

Turning, Waldo met her eyes. For a moment they looked at each other . . . and there was a glow in Delphine's eyes that seemed to trigger a sudden warmth in his heart. He was shaken, almost shocked, by that instinctive response to the friendly warmth in her eyes. Suddenly he knew that he was capable of loving, after all . . . loving very deeply and with all of his being and for all of his life. Suddenly he knew that he loved Delphine very much. Suddenly he was afraid of the tidal wave of emotion that had swept through his life and turned his world upside down and left him a very different man. For the first time in his life, he was at a loss. If they had been alone, he might have taken her hands and smiled into her eyes and told her that he loved her.

But they were not alone. Trevor claimed her attention almost immediately and Charlotte leaned forward to speak, roused from her introspection by that reassuring clasp of his hand. With an effort, Waldo responded, forced himself to be attentive and carefully avoided Delphine's eyes until he was once more in reasonable control of his emotions.

A famous star of stage and television screen, enjoying a late supper with a well-known actress, was coaxed into singing just one song . . . and a round of enthusiastic applause greeted the final note.

Delphine's eyes were wide and very bright with appreciation. She was almost ecstatic in her reception of the song that was currently taking the world by storm.

"Oh, how marvellous!" she breathed as the last note faded into silence.

"He's quite fantastic! I've never heard anyone sing like he does — and it's such a beautiful song. Don't you think so?" She turned instinctively to Waldo, wanting him to share her delight.

He smiled at the glowing eagerness in her face and realized anew how much he loved her and longed to look after her, to keep her with him for the rest of time. "Would you like to meet him?" he asked lightly as the famous singer returned to his table and his companion.

"I should love it," she said promptly. "But wouldn't it be an intrusion?"

"Oh, Daniel and I are old friends," he told her, glad that it was in his power to grant her some small delight. He rose to his feet and held out his hand to her, smiling. "Come along. I'll introduce you."

She went with him, eager and excited, and Trevor looked after her with indulgent affection. He had known Daniel Rush for years and might have effected the introduction. But he had not been as swift as Waldo to perceive the delight that it would give Delphine to meet an internationally famous singer.

Charlotte's slender fingers tightened abruptly on the stem of her empty wine glass and there was a faint spark of annoyance in her eyes. She was irritated by the air of shining innocence which seemed to deceive everyone else so completely. "How you both indulge that child in her whims!" she exclaimed, a little tartly. "You spoil her dreadfully between you."

Trevor poured more wine into her glass. "Some people are a pleasure to spoil," he said smoothly. "Delphine is always so appreciative that I enjoy pleasing her. And so does Waldo, apparently." He looked at her with a flicker of curiosity in his eyes. "Does she seem less of a threat if you emphasize her youth?" he asked lightly.

She gestured impatiently. "She is a child! And not at all your type, Trevor," she added with a swift, provocative smile. "I always thought you liked your women to be rather more sophisticated."

He frowned. "Delphine isn't just one of my women," he told her curtly. "I mean to marry her."

"I don't doubt it. But do you think that she means to marry you?" she returned. "There are moments when she seems to be much more interested in someone else."

He looked at her swiftly, startled, and then amusement leaped to his eyes. "Waldo!" he exclaimed, laughing. "You have to be joking!" He sobered suddenly. "So you do regard her as a threat," he said shrewdly. "Losing your confidence — or is Waldo cooling off? What is it — seven, eight months that you've been together? But you don't really believe that you'll get him to the altar, surely?"

His tone was dry, mocking, faintly cruel. He thought her cold, calculating and much too obvious in her desire for marriage. She was not in love with

Waldo, for she was not a woman who allowed her heart to rule her head. But their engagement had been rumoured so often that it had probably become a matter of pride with Charlotte to turn rumour into fact.

He would be glad to see an end to their relationship. It had lasted longer than was usual with Waldo, and the fact that his name was still being linked with that of Charlotte's after so many months was ominous. There was always a dangerous time in any affair when it seemed easier to drift into marriage than make the break . . . and Trevor had no wish to see his friend married to Charlotte Rivers.

He did not deny her beauty or the quick intelligence or the warm charm which she could use to such effect, but he did not think she was the right wife for Waldo and he had always resisted the speculation about their eventual marriage with a surprising obstinacy. It could not really matter to him if they married. Yet for some odd reason, it did matter, he abruptly discovered. Meeting her green, glowing eyes across the table, he felt the swift stabbing of desire and it suddenly occurred to him that he had always wanted her and refused to admit the truth. Wanting her, he could not accept the thought that she might marry his oldest and closest friend.

The way he felt had nothing to do with loving, of course . . . love was the emotion that Delphine evoked, and he had every intention of marrying Delphine. But he knew that if chance and circumstance ever combined in his favour he would not hesitate to make fierce, demanding love to the beautiful woman who smiled at him now with such infuriating confidence.

"Do you really think that I won't?" she countered lightly, wishing she felt as confident as she forced herself to seem.

Trevor's mouth twisted wryly. "Oh, you have all the weapons and you know how to use them. I've seen you in action, Charlotte! But it could be a mistake to strive for victory simply because you can't face defeat, you know. You'll be cheating yourself as well as Waldo if you marry the title rather than the man. And I'm not convinced that it's the man you want."

Angry colour stole into her face. "I'm not a social climber!" she refuted sharply.

"But you'd enjoy being the Countess of Gildane," he observed. "Almost as much as you'd enjoy the knowledge that you'd beaten all the others at the same game. But it might be a hollow victory, Charlotte — Waldo isn't a man that one cheats with impunity."

★ ★ ★

Music in sentimental mood filled the room as Charlotte placed another record on the stereo. Waldo leaned back in his chair and smiled at her, a little lazily. He was in warm, relaxed mood after a good meal, a glass of fine brandy and a favourite cigar — and it had been a pleasant, easy evening.

"More brandy?" she asked lightly.

"No, thanks." He reached for her hand and drew her towards him and she settled on the thick carpet at his feet, smiling up at him. Her auburn hair curled loosely on her shoulders and she wore a long, colourful caftan. She looked very lovely and much more approachable than usual.

Waldo bent his head to kiss her lightly on the lips. Her arms went swiftly up and about his neck and she melted against him on a rare surge of passion. He abruptly realized that, much as he liked and admired her still, she no longer filled him with the urgent desire that had kept him captive for so long.

He was a little dismayed by this reaction, for it was further evidence of a drastic change in him — and he did not need to look very far for its cause, he thought wryly. Charlotte no longer fired his blood because another woman stirred him to emotions that no man should know for someone who would never belong to him. The way he felt was utterly new and totally devastating and it had shaken him abruptly out of a complacent satisfaction with his way of life.

Alarm coursed through Charlotte as she realized the absence of all desire in his embrace. She clung to him with none of the holding back that she had carefully maintained for months, but he did not quicken with expected response and her heart sank.

She was not in love with this man but she wanted very much to be his wife. Now she knew that the moment had passed when desire might have become loving. Something had happened to change his feelings, just as she had begun to be sure of success.

She had hinted to family and friends that they might soon receive invitations to her wedding. She had started to plan her trousseau. She had dreamed of a future that included a grand society wedding, an extended honeymoon, a return to the lovely manor house in Wiltshire that was Waldo's family home, although he preferred to live in town. She had looked forward with growing confidence to being Lady Gildane.

But now, with Waldo's arm lightly about her waist, she sensed an alteration in his feeling for her. She was going to fail just as had so many other women before her, a fact made all the more bitter because everyone had begun to couple their names automatically and it was generally assumed that they meant to marry. Charlotte shrank from the thought of sympathy from friends and little humiliations from enemies when it became common knowledge that she and Waldo were just good friends, after all.

She did not know if there was some lack in her that failed to inspire Waldo to loving or if it was merely that he was incapable of loving any woman. They were good friends and they were well suited. They had much in common and they enjoyed each other's company and she was sure that she would make him an excellent wife. She did not want to believe that all her hopes were doomed to disappointment but she was too experienced not to recognize the signs that he was drifting away from rather than towards the inclination to marry.

At first, she had been tempted to lay the blame for his growing coolness at his cousin's door. But common sense had soon prevailed. Delphine was not at all his type. He had certainly become fond of the girl but he was much more the benevolent guardian than the ardent admirer. He obviously approved of her romance with Trevor McLean and seemed very ready to hand his cousin into Trevor's keeping. That was hardly the behaviour of a man who wanted the girl for himself.

No, it was much more likely that Waldo had been influenced by the unexpected announcement by friends who had always seemed blissfully happy that they were divorcing. He had been very concerned, very anxious to do what he could to mend matters between the couple without success.

Charlotte had no illusions about Waldo. He might let her down lightly over a period of time, but certainly he would let her down, she thought wryly. Being a proud woman, she decided to break with him before that could happen.

She eased herself gently out of his arms and smiled at him. "I looked in at the gallery this morning," she said carelessly. "It was crowded. I've read some excellent reviews, Waldo."

"Yes, I understand that another three canvases were sold today, all to Americans," he returned lightly. "It was a sound idea of Paul's to time the show with the start of the tourist season. A painting makes a nice souvenir to show the folks back home."

Charlotte laughed. She glanced at the portrait above the mantelpiece, one he had painted in the early days of their friendship and presented to her. "I like so many of your paintings, but that is still my favourite," she said quietly. "Much too flattering, but wonderful for one's ego on a bad day."

Waldo followed her gaze. He studied the painted oval face with detached and critical interest. It was an excellent likeness, exactly capturing the vibrant beauty of the woman. The green of her gown emphasized the extraordinary eyes and complemented the rich auburn of her splendid hair and the creamy warmth of her lovely skin.

He looked from the portrait to the woman by his side, comparing the image with the warm and living reality. She was quite magnificent, he realized anew with a throb of admiration and affection. Working on that portrait of Charlotte, it had crossed his mind that she would make a superb countess with her beauty and elegance and charm. Now it again occurred to him that she would be a worthy addition to the ranks of the Gildanes.

Marriage and Waldo Guthrie had never seemed to have anything in common, until recent events had brought a sudden, sharp awareness that there had to be more to living that the constant pursuit of excitement and adventure and variety. A man grew older, began to think and feel more deeply and thus realized a certain lack in his life.

He had been so sure that no woman could own his mind and heart so completely that life would seem pointless if he could not share it with her till the end of time. He was a proud, confident, light-hearted man and he did not mean to relinquish his freedom or to lose his heart entirely. Yet he had been abruptly humbled by a mere girl who had walked into his life out of the blue.

He could not remember now when he had first been aware of his love for her. It felt as though she had always been a part of his life. He had not wanted to love any woman, but she had stolen into his heart and now he could not imagine a time when he would not love her with all his heart. And every day that passed carried her father from him and closer to the future that she would share with Trevor.

So perhaps he should marry Charlotte and stifle the foolish and so futile longing for Delphine before it held him completely captive. Once he had committed himself to marrying another woman he would not allow himself to dwell on the feelings that Delphine inspired.

Charlotte had much to recommend her as a wife, not least that she was a woman of his own world. She would bring to marriage the quiet resolution that she brought to her successful career. Any marriage that she undertook would succeed simply because she would not allow it to fail. Most of all, she would be content with the little he could give, and she would never know of the yearning within him that only Delphine could ease.

He reached for Charlotte's hand and clasped it warmly. "I didn't do you justice," he said with truth. "It's a portrait of a beautiful woman — and you are so much more than merely beautiful, Charlotte. You have qualities that I couldn't convey because I didn't know you well enough when I painted that portrait. If you sat for me now the result would be very different."

Charlotte smiled wryly. "If I sat for you now, when you know me so much better, you would show the world all my faults."

"If you have any, they are extremely well concealed," Waldo said lightly.

She sent him a laughing glance. "Charmer!"

"No, I mean it. I think you must be the perfect woman," he said, warmth in his eyes and in his voice and in the very attractive smile.

Charlotte eyed him ruefully. "How very boring!"

"If that were true, then I wouldn't be here," he returned. "I've been bored by many women, Charlotte, but never by you."

It was true, for he had always found her an intelligent and stimulating companion. There was a rapport between them which would survive. If he did not marry her, they would continue to be friends, for his admiration and affection for her went very deep.

He suddenly decided to marry her, come what may. He was not at all an impulsive man, so perhaps the idea had been germinating for longer than he knew. Certainly the moment seemed right, now that he had come to terms with his feeling for Delphine and accepted that it had no future. No doubt Charlotte could make him content as long as he resisted the temptation to dream of a happiness he might have known with a girl he loved and would never own.

Wholly unaware of all that was in his mind, Charlotte said quietly: "I think you are beginning to be bored, though, Waldo." She leaned forward to brush her lips against his cheek and smiled into his eyes with an apparently easy candour, but it cost her a great deal to expose herself to almost certain hurt and humiliation.

He carried her hand to his lips, a faint smile lurking in his eyes. "That sounds as though you think I'm losing interest, Charlotte."

"Aren't you?" she countered lightly.

"On the contrary," he returned smoothly. "I've decided to marry you, my dear."

With a little gasp, she went into his arms and gave her lips willingly to his kiss, scarcely able to believe that he had really uttered the words she had begun to suppose she would never hear. It was only later, after he had left her and she had had time to reflect, that she realized the utter arrogance of that announcement.

She was abruptly furious not only with Waldo for the confident assumption that she would leap at the chance of becoming his wife, but also with herself for having reacted with such unbecoming eagerness.

There had been no mention of love, no hint of desire, scarcely a word of affection and certainly not an ounce of regard for her feelings in the matter. He had simply announced his decision to marry her and she had fallen into his arms with a flattering readiness. She was an absolute fool — and she must have handled him very badly all these months for him to be quite so sure of her reaction to those words. He must imagine her to be head over heels in love with him and quite desperate to marry him, while nothing could be farther from the truth. She was not in love with him and not at all certain that she wanted to marry him, after all.

She had virtually got what she wanted, but did she really want it, after all? There was an odd despair in her heart, a little hurt that troubled her because she could not pinpoint its cause. It could not be because Waldo had not once spoken of loving her. She had never wanted nor really expected him to fall in love with her. Yet she felt cheated, she suddenly realized.

Surely there ought to be more to becoming engaged to a man than a cold-blooded declaration of intent on his part and little more than pleased vanity on her part? Surely there ought to be a degree of delight, a hint of happiness for them both in their plans for the future? Waldo had talked of land and property, of settlements, of family matters and legal affairs. He never once referred to the warmth of his regard for her or asked how she felt about him and there had been no shared pleasure in talking about a future that ought to offer happiness and fulfilment.

Charlotte hated hypocrisy and she would have despised him if he had claimed to love her when she knew instinctively that his affection and admiration for her could never amount to the kind of loving a man should feel for the woman he proposed to marry.

He had offered her marriage and she had accepted, so gaining the one thing she was suddenly very inclined to reject. For there ought to be loving on one side at least, and she did not love him any more than he loved her.

It was ironic that she had decided to face up to his growing indifference and bring their affair to an amicable end on the very evening that he had chosen to announce his decision to marry her. She was curious to know what had prompted that decision. It was certainly not overwhelming desire, for no one could have been less ardent than Waldo as he talked quietly and matter-of-factly of marriage settlements.

5

WALDO drove deep into the country despite the lateness of the hour when he left Charlotte. He eventually brought his car to a halt on the brow of a hill and sat for a long time, quietly smoking, reflecting on the past weeks. He stared across the moonlit countryside and saw very clearly the images of two women; the one he loved very dearly and the one he had promised to marry.

He had never been an impulsive man, or he might have been lured into marriage long since, for there had been other women as beautiful, as desirable as Charlotte. He had never wanted to marry any woman until he knew Delphine. He did not really want to marry Charlotte and wondered at that sudden impulse to commit himself to spending the rest of his life with her.

Suddenly it had not seemed to matter very much what he did with his life. Suddenly he had realized the bleak emptiness and lack of purpose that would fill his days when Delphine married and went away from him, although it had seemed that Charlotte might ease his pain and longing. She wanted to marry him and there might be a certain satisfaction in giving her what she wanted. He was aware that she did not love him. Like himself, she had always been level-headed, unemotional, firmly practical in her approach to love and marriage. Whereas his views had changed very rapidly he was sure that Charlotte would be perfectly content with the kind of marriage that he offered. He had heard her described as a woman without a heart and it would suit him very well if that were true, he thought wryly. Charlotte would make no demands on him.

When he finally reached home, the house was in darkness. Although it was very likely that Delphine was tucked into her bed like a good little girl, the house felt empty; empty and unwelcoming and cold. He switched on several lights and stooped to switch on both bars of the electric fire and then poured himself a drink. There was no point in going to bed for he was not likely to sleep on this night of all nights, he thought grimly.

He doubted if there had ever been a newly-engaged man more depressed and chilled by thoughts of the future than himself. He had not set himself an easy task, he realized. Living with himself when he loved a woman who could never belong to him was quite difficult enough without the added problem of living with a woman he had married as an escape.

He stretched out his long legs as he sat in an armchair before the glowing bars of the fire and stared thoughtfully at the amber contents of his glass. He was tormented by the thought of Delphine, asleep in her room, so near to him and yet so impossibly out of reach.

She had looked lovely that evening as she went off with Trevor to dine and dance at a newly-opened night club, her hand linked lightly in the man's arm, her eyes shining with excited, eager anticipation as she looked up at him and then turned to wave farewell as Waldo stood by his car, ready to leave to keep his date with Charlotte. He had felt a stab of envy as Delphine and Trevor drove away, for they seemed so happy, so very confident about the future.

He and Trevor had been close friends since their schooldays and it was impossible to feel animosity towards the man who had won Delphine so easily. But there was a certain constraint between them these days and sometimes he wondered if Trevor was aware that they both wanted the same woman. But Trevor had nothing to fear from him, he thought wryly, knowing it could only be a little time now before he must steel himself for the announcement that Trevor and Delphine were to marry.

Living with Delphine was very difficult at times for he had to force himself to be cool, even distant, in his attitude towards her for fear that a certain warmth in smile or voice or manner might betray the way he felt about her.

Lately, he had seen little of her. He had been busy with the exhibition of his work and other commitments. She had become very popular and her days were filled with social engagements. Sometimes they met only briefly during the day and there had been one day when they had only seen each other because they both went to a certain party. Delphine intruded very little on his life; much too little. At times he wondered if it was a deliberate policy. She was so determined not to be a nuisance, and yet he lived for the rare moments when they were together.

The whisky and the warmth of the

fire combined to make him drowsy. He closed his eyes and drifted into a dream — and it seemed like a fragment of his dream when he became aware of the soft rustle of silk and the trace of drifting perfume.

Delphine looked down at him. All evening she had been troubled by the thought of him and Charlotte together although he spent a great deal of his time with the other woman. Somehow her heart had been very heavy on this particular evening. Looking back at him as she drove away with Trevor, she had known that familiar contraction of her heart and foolishly fancied that he looked a little lost, a little lonely. A foolish fancy, indeed, when he was on his way to spend the evening with the woman he loved, she had rebuked herself. But she had not been able to put him out of her mind and she had been poor company for Trevor. She had pleaded a headache and he was so swiftly solicitous that she had felt guilty. But it would have been impossible to tell him that she was suffering from heartache rather than a headache.

She looked down at Waldo; he looked so vulnerable, so very endearing. She ached to touch her hand to the lock of dark hair that fell across his brow, ached to touch her lips to the lean, bronzed cheek, ached to have his arms about her just once while a certain smile in his eyes that told her she was loved. She sighed, for it was a hopeless dream.

She knew that she was the kind of woman who only loved once in a lifetime and with all her being. Yet it was such a foolish love, she thought wryly. She did not know Waldo half as well as she had come to know Trevor. He had never given her the slightest encouragement to care for him. At times he could be very cold and distant and forbidding and so much a stranger that she wondered if she mistook her feeling for him . . . but the merest hint of his smile was enough to confirm that he was the only man in the world for her.

Love was apparently a law unto itself, ignoring all right, all reason and refusing to allow the very existence of regret. For she had no right to love Waldo when he was probably on the verge of marrying someone else and when she was daily allowing Trevor to grow more fond of her and to think more seriously about a future spent with her. She had no reason to love Waldo when he treated her for the most part with cool, cavalier indifference or avuncular, indulgent tolerance. But there was not an ounce of regret in her heart, for she had found a new awareness of living when she met Waldo and knew that he was her destiny.

She wondered if it would be so wrong, so foolish, to admit to loving him. She suddenly knew a fierce longing to hold him close. She looked down at him with her heart in her eyes, a pulse throbbing heavily in the hollow of her throat. Surely there was no sin in loving? She loved him so much and asked so little in return.

"Waldo," she said softly.

Waldo opened his eyes and looked into her face. He had been so deep in reverie, that he had not heard her come home and he had not really believed that she was there although she had been so vivid, so real to all his senses that it was just as though dream had become reality for the wanting.

Her fragile loveliness caught swiftly at his heart; the slender figure in the soft, clinging silk of her long dress, the small face framed by dark hair, the little smile that sent him tumbling ever deeper into loving in that moment.

He sat up slowly, resisting the instinctive impulse to catch her into him arms. She was much too lovely and much too innocent, and he loved her far too much, he thought wryly.

And he was no longer free to love her, to want her or any other woman, he reminded himself grimly. A man of honour must stifle such impulses when he was newly engaged to Charlotte. Come what may, he must marry the woman to whom he had given his word.

"I must have fallen asleep," he said lightly, brushing the wayward lock back from his forehead and smiling at her lazily. "What time is it? Good grief, time you were in bed, Delphine!" he exclaimed as he discovered it to be close on four o'clock.

"We were rather late," she admitted resenting the tone which instantly relegated her to the position of his cousin and ward and temporary responsibility.

He rose to his feet and stretched to his full height, easing his cramped muscles. "Enjoy yourself?" he asked carelessly.

"Yes, thank you," she said dutifully, but it had not been an enjoyable evening at all. "We had a lot of fun."

He nodded. "Still finding Trevor good company?"

"Yes, of course," she agreed swiftly and that was certainly the truth. She did enjoy Trevor's company and she was very fond of him, but it was not enough to persuade her to marry him. Suddenly she wished that she could explain it all to Waldo; tell him honestly that she only loved him and only wanted to be with him and felt that she cheated Trevor by allowing him to suppose that her affection for him might lead to loving. She had turned more and more to Trevor in the vain hope that he might be able to ease the ache of wanting a man who regarded her with such indifference. She had grown to love Trevor as a dear and valued friend and she had unconsciously encouraged him to care for her and now a proposal was looming and she did not know what to do about it.

Her response was prompt and sincere and yet, glancing at her, Waldo fancied that her eyes were troubled. He was amazingly sensitive to her moods and he knew immediately that she had something on her mind. Perhaps she felt, as he did, that Trevor was taking a very long time to mention marriage although it was obvious that the whole world might know that he was very much in love.

"Is anything wrong?" he asked.

She turned away. "What could be wrong?" she countered swiftly.

Waldo went to her and turned her face towards him, fingers beneath her chin. She looked up at him, her eyes widening, her breath quickening at his unexpected behaviour. He looked down at her, warm understanding in his eyes.

"When a man has the reputation of being a determined bachelor it isn't easy for him to admit that a woman can overcome his instinctive resistance to marriage," he said quietly. "Be patient for just a little longer and I know you'll have what you want, Delphine." He smiled that slow, warm smile. "You would make any man's resistance crumble, after all. You've almost won the day, you know. You'll beat me to the altar yet!"

His first words had caused her heart to leap — and then she realized that he was talking about Trevor rather than himself and she jerked her chin from his fingers and moved away from him so that he should not see the pain of disappointment in her eyes.

She said a little shakily: "You really want me to marry Trevor, don't you?"

"I want you to be happy," he said with sincerity. He looked at her slender back, the dark curls nestling on the nape of her neck, the curve of her cheek as she half-turned her head at his words. "You and Trevor seem to be so right for each other," he went on steadily.

Delphine picked up a heavy glass ornament from a low table and toyed with it, turning it over and over in her hands, studying it so that he should not see the dismay in her eyes.

"Do you really think we are so well-suited?" she asked slowly.

"Ideally matched," he assured her confidently, supposing that she felt all the doubts and fears that were natural to a girl who hovered on the threshold of marriage.

She shook her head. "I don't know," she said then. "I think Trevor would be a marvellous husband — for someone else. The kind of woman who enjoys having her own way in everything, perhaps. I don't think I really like to be spoiled so dreadfully. Trevor does everything to please me. Whatever I want I must have — if I said the sun was in the wrong place for my liking I swear he'd try to have it moved!"

Waldo raised an incredulous eyebrow. "And that's wrong? You're actually complaining?" he asked, laughing. "You're an unusual girl, Delphine!"

She shrugged, a little irritated by his lack of understanding. "I don't want to be treated like a piece of rare porcelain," she said a little desperately. "I don't want to live on a pedestal, admired from a distance and hardly ever touched. That kind of marriage might suit some women, but I should hate it. I want to be treated like a woman," she finished in a rush, the colour stealing into her face.

Waldo felt a little sorry for his friend. Trevor was obviously treading rather too delicately. No doubt he was really in love at last and terrified of doing or saying the wrong thing, anxious not to lose her and equally anxious not to rush her into anything. And all the time Delphine was yearning for the kind of treatment that Trevor had meted out to women in the past. It was really rather ironic, he thought, and wondered why it did not please Delphine to be so loved, so cherished, so respected. After all, she ought to be over the moon with delight that the man she loved was so obviously devoted to her in return.

He smiled and said lightly: "Any man would want to spoil you, Delphine."

The words were lightly-spoken and not to be taken seriously, she knew. Yet her heart quickened, for surely there was a warmth in his eyes that conveyed much more than his tone. She looked at him, her heart beating very fast — and suddenly she threw all discretion to the winds.

"Any man?" she said softly. "How about you, Waldo?"

In a moment, she was in his arms. But he held her much too tightly, so that the buttons of his shirt pressed painfully into her breast. And he kissed her much too fiercely, bruising her mouth and evoking sudden panic.

Quite unprepared for the swift and alarming passion she found in his embrace, she fought him instinctively, her heart filled with sick dismay. For there was no hint of love, of tenderness, in his kiss or his urgent, demanding caresses. He simply wanted her with a fierce, compelling desire that Delphine had never suspected she could arouse in him, although she knew his reputation as a womaniser. She had always supposed herself to be almost too safe with him, for there had never been the least hint of this passion in his attitude all these weeks.

But now there was urgency and intent in the embrace she had so foolishly invited. She had thrown herself at his head on a sudden impulse — and now his blood was on fire and he was very strong, very forceful and very determined.

She knew that she was in very real danger as she struggled in his arms. Not because she really feared he would take her against her will, but because she was so weak with loving and wanting that it would be the easiest thing in the world to surrender to the throbbing urgency of her own desire.

It would be so easy to cease to struggle, to respond with all her being to his need of her — and much too dangerous, she suddenly realized, as her body relaxed in his arms and her lips began to seek his.

With every ounce of her strength, of will as well as body, Delphine forced him away and wrenched herself free and dared him to touch her again with every rigid muscle in her slight figure. "No!" she said jerkily, breathless with wanting and yet furious with him for evoking that betrayal of response and hating him for his empty, superficial desire.

There was an ache within Waldo that was so much more than physical need that he felt her abrupt rejection like a violent blow. Holding her close, knowing the sweetness of her lips, had been greater happiness than he had ever dared to dream. It was intolerable agony that she should wrench herself out of his arms and glare at him so furiously.

She did not understand, he reminded himself. She did not know that he loved her. He held out his hand, a smile just curving his lips, just crinkling his eyes.

"Delphine . . . come back," he said softly, a wealth of tenderness in his eyes.

She shook her head and moved even

farther away from him. She was pale but very determined. She was shaking — and very shaken. All in a moment, she had found a new maturity, for hitherto she had foolishly supposed that only mutual loving could create the kind of magic they had found in each other's arms. She had been so naive, so stupid, she thought bitterly. It was a shock to realize that a man could be in love with one woman and yet know that flooding, compelling desire for another woman. Waldo loved Charlotte and obviously meant to marry her and it ought to be impossible for him to even want to make love to anyone else.

She had led him on, of course. Nothing could have been more stupid or more calculated to lead to such a disastrous situation than her deliberate encouragement. She had thrown herself at him quite unashamedly — and then was startled because a man who was very much a man responded naturally to such an open invitation.

She despised herself for being so helplessly in love that only a moment more would have meant her complete surrender. She despised herself for loving him so much that she could not be angry or humiliated. She despised herself for wanting him so much that her lips throbbed for his kiss and her body ached.

She held out her hands as though to ward him off although he made no move towards her. Waldo's hand fell back to his side and the smile faded from his eyes.

"That shouldn't have happened," Delphine said shakily. "How on earth did it happen, Waldo?"

"Very easily," he said wryly.

"It was all my fault," she said with instinctive candour.

"Yes, I rather think it was your fault," he said dryly. "You shouldn't start anything that you've no desire to finish, Delphine."

The hot blood rushed to her cheeks. "I didn't mean — I mean, I didn't know that you'd react like that," she said defensively.

He looked at her thoughtfully. He loved her and he wanted her very much. But the possession of her lovely, slender body was not all that he wanted. He wanted her love. She had been swift to respond to him, but he must not attach too much importance to that impulse. It was possible to be very much in love and still feel the tug of physical attraction for someone else; and he was sure that Delphine loved Trevor. Perhaps a degree of pique at Trevor's delaying tactics, combined with a natural anxiety that she was not sufficiently desirable, had unconsciously led her to seek reassurance in another quarter. He had been conveniently at hand, Waldo thought wryly. And she had found rather more reassurance than she had expected.

He said: "I'm only human, and you are very lovely. I reacted as any man would to that kind of invitation. And it was an invitation, you know. You wanted to be kissed."

She smiled ruefully, unable to deny the truth in his words. "Kissed — not manhandled!" she countered in light, smiling reproach, striving to dispel any suspicion that his kisses were of any particular importance to her. "I think I'm safer on my pedestal," she added wryly. "At least Trevor doesn't frighten me!"

Trevor had never held her with that kind of urgency, never kissed her with that kind of ardour. Sometimes it had piqued her that he seemed so immune to her feminity. But she knew instinctively that he could never stir her to such depths. It was because she loved Waldo with all her being that she wanted him so much. She must take care never to invite his casual kisses again.

Waldo looked at her swiftly. "Did I frighten you?" he demanded urgently.

"A little . . . " she admitted.

"Oh, Delphine!" he exclaimed. He reached out for her hands and clasped them very tightly, smiling into her eyes with reassurance in his gaze. "Do you suppose I would ever hurt you?" he asked softly. "Heaven forbid!"

Suddenly they were close with a new, warm affinity and understanding. Suddenly her heart lifted with the staggering awareness that he cared just as she cared. Suddenly all the joy and delight of loving and being loved came flooding to fill her being. Suddenly the future was bright with the promise of fulfilment for all her dreams.

She looked up at him happily, a little smile flickering in her eyes. "I'll show you the bruises in the morning!" she said gaily.

"I'll make up for each one," he promised impulsively. He bent to kiss her lightly on lips that unexpectedly flinched from his touch. A frown leaped to his eyes and he tightened his clasp on her hands. "Trust me, Delphine," he said with sudden urgency.

She smiled at him with her heart in her eyes. "I can't trust myself," she said simply, knowing how easy it would be to melt once more into his arms.

A sudden chill struck at his heart. Was it possible that she cared for him and he had been blind and deaf and insensitive to her true feelings all these weeks? More than anything in the world he wanted her love, and yet he was forced to hope that he misunderstood that look in her eyes. For he had promised to marry Charlotte and his word was his bond. It was much too late to discover that he might have spent the rest of his life with the girl he loved so dearly.

Did she love him? He searched her face, his heart hammering with hope even while his head carefully spelled out all the reasons why it was not possible for him to accept that she cared for him.

How could a man tell if a woman loved or if she was merely swept off her feet by the feelings of the moment? All his experience with women in the past was of no use to him now, he thought wryly. He had never wanted to know himself loved and so he had never sought for evidence of love's existence.

Her response to his kisses had been swift and unmistakable, but it did not mean that she loved him. Just now she might be very ready to think herself in love. Just now she was excited, perhaps flattered, certainly eager to believe that the feelings he evoked were born of loving. But in the cold light of day she might feel very differently about him and this brief interlude and he must not take advantage of her present mood when he knew instinctively that certain words were hovering on her lips.

Words were easily spoken and not so easily retracted, he thought wryly. Unless they were truly the key to a future happiness, then he did not want to hear them. He had never told a woman that he loved her. No matter how fierce the heat of the moment or how near he had been to supposing himself in love at last, it had always been part of his personal code that he would never say those words unless he meant them with all his being. He could say them now to Delphine with conviction and absolute dedication — but he was going to marry Charlotte, who would never release him from that impulsive promise of marriage and give him back his freedom.

So he said lightly, carelessly: "Foolish girl. You should kiss me while you can — I shall soon be a married man and quite out of reach, you know!"

Delphine had been expecting it for days. But the light words were still a terrible blow to her loving heart. The colour drained abruptly from her face. There was a rushing in her ears and it took every ounce of her will-power to keep herself from fainting. For this was the end of everything . . . all her hopes, all her dreams, all her instinctive resistance to the thought of his marriage to Charlotte.

She wanted to throw herself into his arms, cling to him desperately, declare that she loved him and could not bear to be without him and that he must not marry anyone but herself. Her heart felt as if it was breaking, her throat ravaged with the tears that she dared not shed. Pride came to her rescue and she heard her own voice saying steadily and with amazing unconcern: "So it's true then? You and Charlotte are getting married? That's wonderful! I'm so happy for you both. Congratulations, Waldo!"

"Thank you," he said, smiling — but the smile did not reach his eyes.

"When is the wedding to be?" she asked.

"We haven't decided on a date yet," he said a little stiffly. "I expect it will be quite soon. We've no reason to delay matters."

"And how do you feel now that your bachelor days are nearly at an end?" she demanded, laughing as though she did not have a care in the world — and wondering how he could be so insensitive to her breaking heart.

"Oh, I'm resigned to my fate," he

returned promptly and with very little truth.

He would marry Charlotte because he must, but he was certainly not resigned to the future even though Delphine could smile and wish him well with a gaiety that utterly dispelled the ridiculous fancy that she might care for him. He must keep his word to Charlotte but it was the knell of despair to realize that Delphine did not love him at all and could witness his marriage to someone else with a light heart.

It had been very foolish to cherish the belief that he had only to want her enough, to be patient enough, for destiny to relent and allow her to belong to him, after all. He had dared to dream an impossible dream . . . and suddenly the dream had crumbled and died. Now there was absolutely no reason why he should not marry Charlotte — and he was bound by honour to do so.

He was still holding Delphine's hands. Now he gave them a slight squeeze and released them. "Time you were in bed, Delphine," he said lightly. He bent down to switch off the bars of the electric fire and then walked to the window, drawing back the heavy drapes to reveal the grey dawn of a new day. "It's almost morning."

Delphine was thankful to escape to her room, and soon she was soaking her pillow with hot, despairing tears as she gave herself up to the heartbreak, the sense of loss, the utter lack of hope for the future. He had never belonged to her and she had always known the futility of loving him — but a girl could dream and she had clung to her dreams for as long as she dared until they were finally dashed from her heart.

Her only comfort lay in the thought that Waldo did not know that she loved him and was mourning for the happiness that she might have known if only destiny had decreed that he love her in return.

Alone once more, Waldo covered his face with his two hands and something very like a groan broke from his lips. He had never felt so much like crying since he was a small boy. To love someone so much when loving promised only frustration and heartache and a longing that could never be eased was almost too much to bear. Now he knew why he had always fought against loving any woman; because he was the kind of man who committed himself utterly to loving.

Abruptly he strode the length of the room to the easel with its covered canvas. This was his newest work and it was concealed from all eyes but his own. He removed the covering and gazed at the almost-finished portrait. He had spent many hours working on this particular canvas. Almost as many hours wrestling with the impulse to destroy it. It was perhaps his greatest work, the one painting that would live long after he was dust — and it was a complete and unmistakable betrayal of his love for the girl he had portrayed.

He had worked diligently on the

portrait, channelling all the love and longing and tenderness into the coming together of hand and eye and brush. In the soft curve of the cheek, the fall of the dark curls, the fragile loveliness of face and figure and the warmth in the shining eyes was all the brilliance of a great artist and all the loving of a mere man.

Waldo gazed at the portrait and wished with all his heart that so much sweetness could belong to him. To be with Delphine, loving her, living only to please and content her was all that he desired — and it was a dream that could never come true. He was to marry Charlotte.

6

IT was a warm and very lovely day and the sun glittered on the tranquil waters of the Serpentine in Hyde Park. Lovers were everywhere, strolling hand in hand, content in the world of their dreams . . . and tearing at Delphine's heart as she watched them and envied them and could not forget the shattering of her own dreams.

The sky was very blue and the grass was very green and the sun was very hot . . . and her heart was very heavy as she sat with Trevor on the sun-soaked terrace of the restaurant that overlooked the lake. She was very grateful for Trevor just now — and not only because their friendship was the camouflage she needed to conceal the way she felt about Waldo and his plans to marry Charlotte.

Trevor made such few demands on

her that she could be at ease with him. She knew that he loved her and wanted to marry her, but he was not urging her into a decision. He had hinted at marriage, but not actually proposed. He had talked of loving her, but so lightly that she did not feel guilty because she was incapable of loving him. He seemed very sure of her affection for him and very sure that she would marry him eventually. He was apparently content to enjoy the present without worrying too much about the future.

Whereas it was the future that concerned Delphine more than anything else. The immediate problem was to find a new roof, she had swiftly realized. It was impossible to live with Waldo any longer, and not only because it was so hard to hide her feelings for him. His engagement to Charlotte had caused a considerable stir and Delphine found it embarrassing to be questioned by reporters who cast obvious doubts on her claim to be Waldo's cousin and smiled and winked knowingly when they discovered that she was his guest. Because of his reputation, her own was suffering. No one seemed to consider it at all unlikely that he had become engaged to one woman while living with another. All her protests and denials had fallen on deaf ears and the last thing she wanted was for the world to suppose that she was Waldo's mistress.

It was added proof, if she had needed it, that she had been very foolish and very naive to come all the way from New Zealand to England with very little money and no security but a relationship to a famous artist with a doubtful reputation. It had been utter madness to throw herself on the hospitality of a distant cousin she had never met. She should have busied herself with finding a job and a place of her own instead of revelling in the excitement of a new country, new friends, a totally new way of life. Certainly she should never have fallen headlong in love with a man completely beyond her reach — that had been the greatest folly of all.

Trevor was silent, thoughtful, the coffee cooling in his cup. Delphine looked at him, a faint frown in her eyes. She did not know what to do. It sounded a simple matter to move out of Waldo's home and into a flat of her own; but only a few weeks of living in London had acquainted her with the fact that it was virtually impossible to find a suitable flat at a rent she could afford anywhere in the metropolis. She would have found life very difficult if she had not been able to rely on Waldo's hospitality, she thought ruefully. Her money had dwindled rapidly since coming to England, for she had spent without giving very much thought to the future. Now there was little left to support her until she found a job — and she could not imagine what kind of work would pay the kind of money she needed to go on living at her present pace. Waldo and Trevor were wealthy men and they had introduced her into circles where money was important because there was always plenty of it. Delphine shrank from admitting that she was virtually penniless by comparison.

She toyed with the idea of returning to New Zealand. But she loved London and liked England and had swiftly come to regard it as her new home. And even if she could not be with Waldo it was some small comfort to know that she would see him from time to time. It was perhaps the only advantage in being related to him, she thought wryly.

There was a very simple solution to all her problems, of course. She could marry Trevor. She was very fond of him and she supposed it might be possible to find a degree of happiness as his wife. It was probably foolish to feel that even the thought of marrying another man seemed an act of disloyalty to her love for Waldo. It was all very well feeling that she would sooner starve; that might well be the alternative.

She laid her hand tentatively on Trevor's arm and he turned to her with his ready smile.

"Sorry, I was a million miles away," he said lightly. "What did you say?"

"I didn't speak. I just wanted to bring you back," she said, smiling. "I believe you'd forgotten all about me."

He covered her hand swiftly with his own. "Impossible!" he declared. He added with truth: "You were very much in my thoughts, actually."

"Penny for them?" she offered.

He laughed and shook his head. "Not for sale . . . not at any price!" He rose to his feet and smiled down at her. "Come on, let's walk. It might be cooler by the water."

They strolled hand in hand by the lake like lovers — and Delphine wished that she could love him. Life would be so much easier, so much happier, so much more secure, she thought wistfully.

Trevor was very conscious of the

slight girl at his side. He turned his head to glance at her and she looked up with a swift, warm smile — and he wondered that he had ever supposed that he loved her. She was very sweet, very appealing — and he did not love her in the least. Not as a man should love the woman he had seriously thought of marrying, anyway.

It was not in character for him to be swept off his feet by a woman. Yet only a few hours with Delpine had convinced him that he was in love at last and eager for marriage. The feeling had stayed with him for weeks — and then died a sudden and unexpected death. Now he knew that whatever he had felt for Delphine it had not been love. Now he knew that he could never marry her. He felt tender and very protective towards her. He shrank from hurting and disappointing her and her happiness was very important to him. But he could never marry her — and he was thankful that some instinct had kept him from committing himself completely.

He marvelled that he could have been so blind to the truth for so long. He had wasted an awful lot of time and energy in resisting the inevitable. He had refused to recognize his feeling for Charlotte until it was almost too late. He had known that she had a considerable impact on his emotions but he had attributed it all to physical attraction, and it was only now that he realized how small a part desire actually played in his feelings for her. He wanted to marry her and he was determined to do so if he had to trample on the entire world to get what he wanted.

He did not know why Waldo had suddenly decided to settle down or why he had chosen to marry Charlotte when any fool could tell that he was not the least in love. But Trevor felt that there had to be a way to prevent such an unsuitable marriage from taking place. Waldo was not really the marrying kind, after all. He would make Charlotte miserable within six months.

Delphine smiled up at him warmly and knew a sudden rush of affection for him. There could be many worse fates for a girl in her position than marriage to a man so nice, so kind, so understanding, she thought impulsively. Perhaps in time she could overcome the folly of loving Waldo and learn to care with all her heart for the man who loved her and surely wanted to marry her and would certainly look after her so well.

"I do love you!" she said in a little rush, clinging tightly to his hand. "Oh, Trevor, couldn't we get married? I should feel so safe with you."

He stopped in his tracks and stared down at her, taken aback. Only a few days before he would have thought himself the happiest of men to hear such words, he thought wryly. Now he was dismayed. "Get married . . . ?" he echoed, playing for time, not quite knowing what to say, what to do.

"Please . . . " she said softly, reaching

up to kiss him lightly on the lips. "Very soon, Trevor!"

Her eyes were bright and trusting. She looked at him as though he were every inch a god and a hero . . . and he felt like the lowest of the low in that moment. For he had allowed her to believe that he loved her. He had urged her to love him. He had courted her with all the intent of a man determined on marriage. And now that he knew without a shadow of doubt that Charlotte was the only woman in the world for him, Delphine had chosen to fall in love with him.

He looked away, disconcerted and shaken. "What a place to propose to a man!" he exclaimed, taking refuge in flippancy. "This is so sudden!"

Delphine abruptly realized that he was not reacting as she had expected. Here was no delighted lover finding all his dreams coming true. He was embarrassed and dismayed and completely at a loss. So it seemed that he did not love her, after all. All his references to love and marriage and sharing the future with her had been so much empty talk. She was rapidly coming to the conclusion that no man could be trusted. It seemed that every one of them found it easy and amusing to play fast and loose with woman's feelings. It seemed every man was content to indulge in light-hearted affairs and quick to panic as soon as one threatened to become too serious, too demanding. It seemed that even Trevor was going to fail her when she needed him most.

It did not matter, of course. She had half-regretted those impulsive words as soon as they were spoken and now she knew that she did not want to marry a man she did not and would never love, come what may. But it hurt that he was reluctant when she had been so sure that he loved and wanted her. She supposed there must be some lack in her that made it impossible for any man to feel a lasting love for her.

"Too sudden," she said slowly. "And

it isn't what you want, anyway." She smiled at him a little tremulously. "I'm sorry. I didn't mean to embarrass you, Trevor."

"Oh, Delphine . . . " he said, quite helplessly.

Now he knew even less what to say. Unshed tears sparkled in her eyes and it was obvious that he had hurt her badly and that was the last thing he had wanted.

"You mean a great deal to me . . . " he began a little lamely, and trailed off uncertainly.

Delphine searched his troubled face. "But you don't want to marry me," she announced steadily.

He winced at the blunt statement of fact. "I don't know what to say . . . how to explain," he tried again, convinced that her heart must be breaking and admiring the courage which compelled her to face facts so quietly.

"All you have to say is that you've fallen out of love," she said lightly. "It happens — and it isn't the end of the world."

He touched his hand to her cheek in a swift, reassuring gesture. "I expect it feels that way just now, though," he said gently. Suddenly he put an arm about her shoulders and drew her to walk along at his side once more. For one thing, they were attracting attention; for another, he found it easier to talk to her if he did not meet the pain and bewilderment in her eyes.

"I can't bear to hurt you," he said ruefully. "I've behaved like a fool and I've no defence. I thought I loved you and I rushed my fences and that was very wrong. I've encouraged you to care for me and now I have to admit that I can't marry you, Delphine. You see, there's someone else . . . I'm in love with someone else," he admitted rather unsteadily. It was the first time he had actually spoken of his feeling for Charlotte and words suddenly seemed hopelessly inadequate.

Delphine looked at him quickly, surprised — and yet his words were only confirmation of something she had instinctively known without realizing that she knew. For a man as much in love as he had seemed to be surely could not be content to admire and adore from a distance — and yet there had never been anything more than an occasional friendly hug, a casual kiss, linked hands and shared smiles, the warm exchange of affection and friendship. He had loved her only as a friend and dear companion . . . as she had loved him.

"Why didn't you tell me?" she asked slowly. "You know I'd have understood, Trevor."

He smiled a wry little smile. "I didn't know myself until this week — and if that sounds crazy, I can't help it. It's the truth."

"This week?" she echoed and her heart gave a little leap of excitement. "Trevor, is it Charlotte?" she asked swiftly, perceptively. "Are you in love

185

with Charlotte?"

"Yes . . . for my sins," he agreed grimly.

"Oh, Trevor!" she exclaimed shakily. "Can't you persuade her not to marry Waldo?"

Once more he stopped in his tracks and looked down at her. There was something in her eyes that told him all that he should have realized long since. "I'll do my best," he said slowly. "For both our sakes . . . !" He caught her into his arms and held her close, comfortingly. "We are a couple of fools, aren't we?" he declared ruefully. "You want Waldo and I want Charlotte — and we'd probably be a darned sight happier with each other!"

Later, after he had taken Delphine home and left her with the assurance that if it was in his power she should have all the happiness she deserved, Trevor made his way resolutely across London in search of Charlotte. He was fortunate in finding her at home for she had stayed away from the office since the announcement of her engagement with all its attendant publicity.

She opened the door to Trevor with faint surprise. He was not in the habit of calling on her. Indeed, he was much more likely to go out of his way to avoid her, she thought dryly.

"I want to talk to you," he announced without ceremony.

She led the way into the lounge. "Feel free . . . " she said lightly. She sat down on a sofa and leaned back against the cushions, regarding him curiously. "This is most unexpected," she added, quite unable to conceal her surprise. Her eyes narrowed abruptly. "Is anything wrong . . . is it Waldo?" she demanded, straightening with sudden alarm as he stood silent and seemingly tense.

"He's fine, as far as I know. I haven't seen him for a couple of days." Trevor sat down and took his cigarette case from his pocket. His hands shook a little as he extracted a cigarette and put it between his lips. It had seemed a simple matter to walk into her flat and announce that he had no intention of allowing her to marry Waldo. Suddenly it seemed the most colossal cheek. He could scarcely expect her to break her engagement just because he loved her with all his heart, he thought wryly. And yet he could not believe that she cared deeply for Waldo. She was merely set on achieving an ambition and that was not really worthy of a woman like her.

Charlotte relaxed. She smiled at him — the warm, glowing smile that she bestowed on every man without ever giving a thought to its impact. She knew that she was beautiful and desirable and much admired but she was not consciously provocative.

Trevor looked at her, unsmiling. He snapped his lighter to flame and drew deeply on his cigarette. "So you're engaged to Waldo," he said abruptly.

She raised an eyebrow at his tone. "For once you may believe what you read in the newspapers," she returned airily. "Yes, I'm engaged to Waldo."

"Why?"

Charlotte stiffened. "I imagine that must be obvious," she said lightly.

"Very obvious," he observed.

The merest hint of colour stole into her face. "I'm very fond of Waldo," she said, on the defensive and wondering why it was necessary to defend her behaviour at all. It was nothing to do with Trevor or anyone else if she married Waldo with or without love, she thought impatiently. Yet the look in his eyes, partly accusation, partly reproach made her feel oddly guilty. He had never liked her, of course. He had never thought her capable of real love for Waldo. She did not know why she should care for his good opinion and yet this was the one person she had dreaded to meet since her engagement was announced. She had expected to see just that look of condemnation in Trevor's eyes but anticipation did not soften the shock of dismay.

Trevor knew without question that

he would always love her. Love had its reasons for linking one man with one woman with invisible and unbreakable bonds — but loving did not guarantee happiness or fulfilment. It was foolish to fight one's destiny and so he accepted that he would love Charlotte for ever . . . but he was also forced to accept that loving her did not give him any right to a place in her heart for life.

"Do you think that's enough?" he asked tautly.

Charlotte was troubled by the strange, near-to-snapping tension in a man she had tried so hard to dislike because he had always appeared to dislike and despise her. Yet she did not dislike him at all, she realized abruptly. In some strange way he was very important and she had always desperately wanted his liking and approval while striving to appear wholly indifferent.

"I know what you think of me, Trevor," she said slowly and with a hint of regret in her tone. "But I do mean to make him happy, you know."

"And will you be happy?" he demanded abruptly, and saw something flicker in her eyes. A little shadow of doubt, perhaps. Or surprise at a concern that he had never previously betrayed. "Waldo isn't the easiest of men, you know," he added.

Charlotte did know. Waldo was not an artist for nothing and there were times when nothing mattered but his work and he was utterly ruthless in dismissing the personal from his life. She was aware that being married to him would not be a bed of roses. Perhaps if he loved her . . . or if she loved him . . . ? The woman who married Waldo would need to be very loving and giving and adaptable to his moods and needs. She doubted if she fitted that description. She was much too intelligent and demanding, she thought wryly.

"I'm not the easiest of women," she returned with a rueful laugh. "I expect

191

Waldo and I deserve each other!"

"I doubt if you love each other," he said quietly.

"No," she said honestly. "I don't think we do. I didn't think it mattered . . . but now I'm not so sure." She smiled at him suddenly, warmly. "I don't think I know what I want any more, Trevor."

He stubbed his cigarette and rose to his feet. He looked down at her, smiling. It was a smile of such exceptional sweetness that Charlotte caught her breath and her heart gave an unexpected throb of gladness.

"I know what I want," he said quietly and with unmistakable meaning. He bent down and put both arms about her and drew her to her feet and looked deep into her glowing eyes. "I want you, Charlotte — so much," he told her softly. "I can't make you a countess, my darling. Will you settle for being a much-loved Mrs. Trevor McLean?"

Charlotte suddenly knew why she had

felt so cheated when she found herself engaged to Waldo almost against her will. He had utterly failed to make her feel that she was loved. She was merely a beautiful and desirable object that he had decided to acquire and her feelings in the matter had not really interested him. Suddenly it was very important indeed that she should be loved . . . and there was a wealth of meaning in Trevor's eyes that told her how much he loved and needed her and always would.

"Anyone can be a countess," she said a little tremulously. She raised her face for his kiss with a joyous conviction that this was right for both of them . . .

★ ★ ★

Waldo was working, putting the finishing touches to a canvas, concentrating so intently on the final strokes that he was not immediately aware of Delphine's entry into the room.

She paused by the door, reluctant to disturb him, knowing that he hated to be interrupted when he was working. She stood looking at the tall and handsome man who was so very dear to her and there was a heaviness touching her heart. It would be very wrong to slip away without saying good-bye to him — but it was going to be so hard, she thought unhappily.

She had quite made up her mind to go. She had no plans, but it was obvious that she must not stay with Waldo any longer. It had been a mistake to turn up on his doorstep without invitation in the first place. But she could not have known that she was going to fall so deeply in love with him. She would learn to live with her love for him, but she could not live with him any longer. Besides, he would soon be married to Charlotte and bringing his bride to this house and it obviously would be impossible for her to share the same roof as Waldo and his wife. It was wise to go as soon as possible and try to put her love for him out of her heart and mind.

She must face up to the fact that there was no future in loving him. She had always known it but her stubborn heart had persisted in hoping and dreaming all these weeks. Even now she was clinging to the foolish hope that Trevor might have some influence with the woman he had gone to see as soon as he left her earlier in the day. But Charlotte was probably quite determined to marry Waldo and she was not likely to consider Trevor as a possible husband when she had received Waldo's proposal first. But even if Waldo's engagement did collapse through one cause or another there was not the least likelihood that he would ever turn to her, Delphine thought ruefully. All the loving, all the hoping, all the dreaming in the world could not bring about the miracle.

She set down her suitcase and moved further into the room. She meant to find a quiet hotel for a few days while she worked out her future. She had imposed on Waldo far too long and it was much more sensible to do something constructive with her life instead of fretting for something she could never have.

Waldo turned, suddenly aware of her. "What is it?" he asked abruptly. He had been so absorbed in his work that he found it difficult to adjust his mood to the moment.

Delphine hesitated. "I'm disturbing you . . ."

"Yes. What do you want?"

His tone was forbidding and Delphine felt rebuffed. But she took another step towards him, needing to lessen the distance between them. His tall frame had been blocking the easel, but as she drew nearer the vivid, glowing colours of the canvas caught her eye. She stared, her eyes widening in amazement.

"Waldo! My portrait!" she exclaimed impulsively.

Instinctively he snatched up a cover

to throw over the canvas. He had not meant to show her the portrait and he did not want her to recognize the intense emotion that had gone into every stroke of the brush. For what good could it do now for her to know that he loved her?

Delphine checked his hand. "Do let me look!" she said urgently. Waldo shrugged and turned away, resigned to the inevitable.

She stood by the easel, studying the glowing portrait, taken aback and oddly disturbed and marvelling all at the same time. She was astonished by its very existence when she had supposed him to have lost interest in the idea of painting her. She was impressed with the artistic skill which had given such glowing life to a mere painting. But she was looking at a stranger, she thought, staring at the girl who smiled back at her with such shining eyes, such sweetness of expression.

"I didn't know you were doing this," she said slowly, wondering. "I thought you'd changed your mind about it. I only sat for you a couple of times."

Waldo went to a side-table and poured himself a drink. "I didn't need you," he said carelessly — and did not dare to recall the many times when he had needed her with a desperate and dangerous intensity and kept her firmly at a distance because he did not trust his emotions not to betray him. "I do have a pretty good idea of what you are like, even if I am only treated to very brief glimpses of you these days."

She turned to look at him with troubled eyes. "It's me — but it isn't me at all, Waldo," she told him quietly.

A little smile came to his lips. "It's very much you, Delphine."

She shook her head. "It's not the person that I see in the mirror!"

He was abruptly moved to tenderness by that instinctive modesty. But he merely laughed and said lightly: "You have to allow for artistic licence, Delphine."

"I know so little about art that I've

no right to criticize. But I don't really like it, Waldo. Do you mind?" she said, a little anxiously.

She was always so honest, he thought wryly. It could be refreshing. It could also be hurtful. But he would not have her any different, he decided.

"Not at all," he told her, smiling. "I don't paint to please other people, not even the people I paint."

Perhaps it was just as well that she did not understand what it was about the portrait that she did not like or understand. For once she was not as perceptive as he had feared she would be and she did not realize that he had been looking through the eyes of love when he painted the portrait of her.

She moved to his side swiftly and caught his hand. "I've hurt you. I'm sorry!" she said impulsively. "My tactless tongue!"

"You don't have to like it," he said, smiling. "But I do. It's the best thing I've ever done."

Her eyes widened. "Truly?"

He nodded. "I think so."

Her face was suddenly alight with pleasure. "I'm glad — if you really mean it," she said a little shyly.

She looked so sweet that it took all his resolution not to draw her into his arms and hold her very close to his heart. He said lightly: "I shall send it to the gallery and we'll see if the experts agree with you or with me."

"They won't know the real me," she said swiftly. "So they won't see that it isn't true." She struggled to express her feeling about the portrait. "I know we all look through different eyes. But I'm not really the girl in the portrait, Waldo." She added wistfully: "She looks the kind of person I'd like to be . . . and never could be!"

Waldo abruptly lifted the hand within his own to his lips and there was warmth and tenderness in his eyes as he looked into her face.

"Dear Delphine," he said softly, and her name was an endearment. "An artist has to be true to his inner eye.

I painted what I saw. Believe me, you are the girl in the portrait — a lovely and very lovable person." He bent to touch his lips to her cheek — so gently, so fleetingly that it was barely a kiss.

Delphine's heart stood still . . . and then plunged with despair. It was such a light, meaningless, cousinly kiss, and the warmth in his words was only the warmth of the careless, indulgent affection such as he had always shown towards her.

She did not know that Waldo was keeping a very tight rein on his feelings and that it was almost too much to ask of him to resist the aching need for her nearness, her warm and yielding response to his loving.

Disappointment flooded her when he drew back, smiling, untouched by any of the heady emotions that gripped her so fiercely. She took refuge in flippancy, saying lightly: "Now don't waste kisses on me, Waldo. I still don't like the portrait."

He laughed a little ruefully. She had

not exactly rejected the touch of his lips but she had certainly not welcomed nor responded to the light kiss that was all that he had dared. He felt suddenly reckless. Nothing venture, nothing gain . . . and he could not go meekly into marriage with another woman without having known again the delight of Delphine's loveliness in his arms.

"Perhaps I can persuade you to change your mind," he said softly, a little mischievously. "I can be very persuasive, you know . . . "

She backed away hastily. "Waldo, I only came in to say good-bye . . . "

The telephone shrilled as she spoke. Waldo looked at her, frowning. "Good-bye?" he echoed. "What does that mean?"

The telephone shrilled again.

"I'm going away," she said carefully.

The strident summons of the telephone was very persistent.

"Where are you going?" he demanded brusquely. "What are you talking about, Delphine?"

Unable to bear it any longer, Delphine silenced the telephone by picking up the receiver and giving the number.

"Waldo . . . Yes, he's here. Hold on!" She held the receiver out to him. "It's Charlotte," she said stiffly.

He took the receiver, impatient at the interruption. "Hello . . . Charlotte? I'm very busy just now. All right — yes, I'm listening!"

Delphine stood irresolute for a moment. Then she reached to kiss his lean cheek, her heart pounding. Instantly she turned away, eluding the hand that reached instinctively to detain her. She smiled at him with rueful love in her eyes, thinking of how much she cared for him and what might have been if only destiny had decreed that he might love her in return. Waldo frowned back at her, trying to concentrate on Charlotte's voice and wishing her at the bottom of the sea at that particular moment, for he had the most incredible suspicion that Delphine's eyes were telling him something that he had only dared to dream.

Abruptly he realized exactly what it was that Charlotte was saying and he swiftly covered the mouthpiece and said urgently: "Delphine . . . don't dare to slip away! I have to talk to you!"

She shook her head and picked up her suitcase with obstinacy in her eyes. She had to go and there was no point in delaying matters. It only deepened the despair in her heart and mind.

Waldo said hastily into the telephone as she crossed the room with obvious purpose: "Charlotte, it's marvellous . . . I'm delighted for you both. Be happy. Tell me all about it when you get back from your honeymoon!"

He slammed down the receiver and went after Delphine and caught her as she reached the head of the narrow staircase.

He put his hand on her shoulder and spun her round to face him — and she dropped the heavy suitcase, which flew open and scattered her clothes all over the floor and the stairs.

"Oh, Waldo . . . !" she wailed.

"Never mind. You aren't going anywhere," he told her firmly.

He put his arms about her and drew her close and rested his cheek on her dark hair . . . and for the first time in weeks his heart and mind were at peace. Delphine stood in his embrace and it was just like coming home, she thought thankfully, not knowing how the miracle had come about but glad with all her heart. For the moment they were content to hold each other, to know that they shared the same delight in that togetherness.

"I love you," he said at last, those three simple words filled with meaning from the very depths of his being. "I love you and I can't let you leave me," he told her.

"Oh, Waldo . . . " She sighed, for there were no words to express how she felt in that moment.

He drew back to look at her, to look deeply into the shining eyes. "Charlotte has jilted me — for Trevor," he said quietly, thankfully. "I gather that it comes as no surprise to you?"

"I thought it might happen and dreaded it for your sake," she said honestly. "I thought you would be terribly hurt."

He smiled wryly. "And I thought you loved Trevor. How could you put me through such torment all these weeks!"

"You seemed to want me to care for him, and I only wanted to please you," she said gravely. "How could I know that you wanted me when everyone was so sure that you meant to marry Charlotte? Do you really want me, Waldo? As your wife, I mean?" she added. "I — I'm a very ordinary girl."

"You're my kind of girl," he told her firmly. "Not at all ordinary. Wholly delightful and eternally dear and I shall always love you. Of course I want you for my wife — but are you really sure that you want me for a husband?"

"With all my heart," she said simply.

Waldo caught her close, overwhelmed with love for her and the incredible realization that the dear delight that was Delphine was his to have and to hold for ever.

He kissed her gently, tenderly. The touch of his lips was the promise of happiness, the golden key to a new world wherein all the dreams that they had ever dared to dream would come true . . .

THE END

Other titles in the Linford Romance Library:

A YOUNG MAN'S FANCY
Nancy Bell

Six people get together for reasons of their own, and the result is one of misunderstanding, suspicion and mounting tension.

THE WISDOM OF LOVE
Janey Blair

Barbie meets Louis and receives flattering proposals, but her reawakened affection for Jonah develops into an overwhelming passion.

MIRAGE IN THE MOONLIGHT
Mandy Brown

En route to an island to be secretary to a multi-millionaire, Heather's stubborn loyalty to her former flatmate plunges her into a grim hazard.

WITH SOMEBODY ELSE
Theresa Charles

Rosamond sets off for Cornwall with Hugo to meet his family, blissfully unaware of the shocks in store for her.

A SUMMER FOR STRANGERS
Claire Hamilton

Because she had lost her job, her flat and she had no money, Tabitha agreed to pose as Adam's future wife although she believed the scheme to be deceitful and cruel.

VILLA OF SINGING WATER
Angela Petron

The disquieting incidents that occurred at the Vatican and the Colosseum did not trouble Jan at first, but then they became increasingly unpleasant and alarming.

DOCTOR NAPIER'S NURSE
Pauline Ash

When cousins Midge and Derry are entered as probationer nurses on the same day but at different hospitals they agree to exchange identities.

A GIRL LIKE JULIE
Louise Ellis

Caroline absolutely adored Hugh Barrington, but then Julie Crane came into their lives. Julie was the kind of girl who attracts men without even trying.

COUNTRY DOCTOR
Paula Lindsay

When Evan Richmond bought a practice in a remote country village he did not realise that a casual encounter would lead to the loss of his heart.

ENCORE
Helga Moray

Craig and Janet realise that their true happiness lies with each other, but it is only under traumatic circumstances that they can be reunited.

NICOLETTE
Ivy Preston

When Grant Alston came back into her life, Nicolette was faced with a dilemma. Should she follow the path of duty or the path of love?

THE GOLDEN PUMA
Margaret Way

Catherine's time was spent looking after her father's Queensland farm. But what life was there without David, who wasn't interested in her?

HOSPITAL BY THE LAKE
Anne Durham

Nurse Marguerite Ingleby was always ready to become personally involved with her patients, to the despair of Brian Field, the Senior Surgical Registrar, who loved her.

VALLEY OF CONFLICT
David Farrell

Isolated in a hostel in the French Alps, Ann Russell sees her fiancé being seduced by a young girl. Then comes the avalanche that imperils their lives.

NURSE'S CHOICE
Peggy Gaddis

A proposal of marriage from the incredibly handsome and wealthy Reagan was enough to upset any girl — and Brooke Martin was no exception.

A DANGEROUS MAN
Anne Goring

Photographer Polly Burton was on safari in Mombasa when she met enigmatic Leon Hammond. But unpredictability was the name of the game where Leon was concerned.

PRECIOUS INHERITANCE
Joan Moules

Karen's new life working for an authoress took her from Sussex to a foreign airstrip and a kidnapping; to a real life adventure as gripping as any in the books she typed.

VISION OF LOVE
Grace Richmond

When Kathy takes over the rundown country kennels she finds Alec Stinton, a local vet, very helpful. But their friendship arouses bitter jealousy and a tragedy seems inevitable.

CRUSADING NURSE
Jane Converse

It was handsome Dr. Corbett who opened Nurse Susan Leighton's eyes and who set her off on a lonely crusade against some powerful enemies and a shattering struggle against the man she loved.

WILD ENCHANTMENT
Christina Green

Rowan's agreeable new boss had a dream of creating a famous perfume using her precious Silverstar, but Rowan's plans were very different.

DESERT ROMANCE
Irene Ord

Sally agrees to take her sister Pam's place as La Chartreuse the dancer, but she finds out there is more to it than dyeing her hair red and looking like her sister.

HEART OF ICE
Marie Sidney

How was January to know that not only would the warmth of the Swiss people thaw out her frozen heart, but that she too would play her part in helping someone to live again?

LUCKY IN LOVE
Margaret Wood

Companion-secretary to wealthy gambler Laura Duxford, who lived in Monaco, seemed to Melanie a fabulous job. Especially as Melanie had already lost her heart to Laura's son, Julian.

NURSE TO PRINCESS JASMINE
Lilian Woodward

Nick's surgeon brother, Tom, performs an operation on an Arabian princess, and she invites Tom, Nick and his fiancé to Omander, where a web of deceit and intrigue closes about them.

THE WAYWARD HEART
Eileen Barry

Disaster-prone Katherine's nickname was "Kate Calamity", but her boss went too far with an outrageous proposal, which because of her latest disaster, she could not refuse.

FOUR WEEKS IN WINTER
Jane Donnelly

Tessa wasn't looking forward to meeting Paul Mellor again — she had made a fool of herself over him once before. But was Orme Jared's solution to her problem likely to be the right one?

SURGERY BY THE SEA
Sheila Douglas

Medical student Meg hadn't really wanted to go and work with a G.P. on the Welsh coast although the job had its compensations. But Owen Roberts was certainly not one of them!

HEAVEN IS HIGH
Anne Hampson

The new heir to the Manor of Marbeck had been found. But it was rather unfortunate that when he arrived unexpectedly he found an uninvited guest, complete with stetson and high boots.

LOVE WILL COME
Sarah Devon

June Baker's boss was not really her idea of her ideal man, but when she went from third typist to boss's secretary overnight she began to change her mind.

ESCAPE TO ROMANCE
Kay Winchester

Oliver and Jean first met on Swale Island. They were both trying to begin their lives afresh, but neither had bargained for complications from the past.

CASTLE IN THE SUN
Cora Mayne

Emma's invalid sister, Kym, needed a warm climate, and Emma jumped at the chance of a job on a Mediterranean island. But Emma soon finds that intrigues and hazards lurk on the sunlit isle.

BEWARE OF LOVE
Kay Winchester

Carol Brampton resumes her nursing career when her family is killed in a car accident. With Dr. Patrick Farrell she begins to pick up the pieces of her life, but is bitterly hurt when insinuations are made about her to Patrick.

DARLING REBEL
Sarah Devon

When Jason Farradale's secretary met with an accident, her glamorous stand-in was quite unable to deal with one problem in particular.